Abe Wallace
U.S.
Federal Marshal

In Pursuit of a Madman

LIVE THE WILD WEST

Orin Vaughn

D1529044

DEDICATION

To the memory of my Pop and Uncle Al

ACKNOWLEDGMENTS

I have published this book in the belief that there are still those out there who appreciate a Western written in the Classic, Traditional Style. No, I do not claim to be the quality of writer as those before me, who you and I admire. However, neither do I want their style and tradition to be forgotten or lost.

Volumes and volumes of Western Stories have been written and read, some GREAT, others not so great. Western books have been given as gifts, passed around, traded, and sold at yard sales and to used bookstores. Still, they are picked up by a *select few* and read and reread and passed around again.

So, hopefully here is a New Story for you, with the same flavor that some of us still appreciate.

Yours truly,
ORIN VAUGHN

Thanks to my friends, family and Mike Brose, Greg Middleton and Nick Wale.

Some Cover Art thanks to the excellent talents of Jim Hagstrom.

Preface

Abraham Francis Wallace, was born to Francis Albert and Ruth Ann (Cook) Wallace, on February 12, 1839. The Wallace's were Illinois farmers on 60 acres of good soil, that they worked with Francis' brother Stanley and his family, all worked hard and did well.

Abraham's mother Ruth, died just a week after his third birthday. She was gored and trampled to death by a nasty natured bull, Abe's father had just purchased for breeding. Francis, without hesitation shot the expensive animal immediately, but it was too late for Ruth, she died in his arms. Francis' never remarried, instead he dedicated himself to the farm and hard work. He wasn't a bad father as far as providing was concerned, however, the only loving care young Abraham got was from his Aunt Susie, which fortunately tempered, the demanding, unsympathetic treatment of his father.

Abe was 15 when his father died of a heart attack while plowing in the fields. After that, Abe quickly grew tired of farming and wanted to pursue something different in life, so he decided to leave the farm in mid-state Illinois. He left everything in Stanley's care and moved in with an uncle in Peoria, Illinois.

Abe admired his uncle Bob, who was a city constable, a man of principle and high regards for law and justice, which was picked up and absorbed by his young impressionable nephew. Abe even served as a constable himself until he joined the Union Army in '62 and in short order earned Sargent stripes in an artillery unit. The war taught Abe some hard and serious lessons about life and death.

After the war, Abe didn't go back to Illinois, he went West and joined the Texas Rangers. In 1867, he became a US Deputy Marshal in South West Texas, and was later sent to Arizona Territory. Abe, built a reputation as a skillful lawman, assisting in the apprehension of a number of dangerous desperados and murders.

In 1870, he was offered, one of a few appointed commissions as a US Federal Marshal. This appointment gave him jurisdiction in any state or territory in the borders of the United States. Abe served and built a reputation as a man of unquestionable resolve, one who would get his man, no matter what it took.

Abe, had never killed a man in cold blood, a

madman like Balestine was different though.

Abe Wallace, US Federal Marshal

The morning sun cut brilliant, colorful paths of gold light through the fall trees; there was however, a cold, wet, chill in the air. Abe sat leaning back against a large bolder, just 30 or so yards from where Balestine rested comfortably in the little trapper's cabin down the hill. Abe balanced the thin cheroot he had just lit, to help keep him awake, on a small flat rock and unstopped his whisky flask. He took a long pull from the flask, dribbles ran down his chin and over a week's growth of facial hair around his mouth. The ground he was sitting on was damp and clammy. It sure would be nice to spend just one night in the soft, feather bed at Mavis May's place. The chilled air caused phlegm to build up in his throat and he had to cough shallow a few times. He held it back, so as not to make any more noticeable noise than was forced out, beyond his control.

Finally, he had caught up with the heartless, murdering, hunk of useless flesh, Salmon Balestine. Abe had no intentions of letting him get away this time, except maybe over his dead body. He certainly wouldn't mind ridding the world of him with just the slightest provocation. Unable to start any kind of a fire, without giving himself away, Abe huddled up in his heavy corduroy coat with the buffalo hair collar. He was glad he had bought it when he did, back at Happy Jack's Trading Post. It kept him fairly warm from the frosted morning cold. As he sat there, he took another swig from his whiskey flask, then he slipped it back into the inside pocket of his vest and closed his eyes, just for a minute—

Nick, Abe's mustang sensed the movement down at the cabin before he did. The horse was tethered nearby and his ears were forward and his eyes watched attentively. Abe had owned him about eight years, Nick was an exceptionally perceptive animal, he seemed to read Abe's mind at times. Abe peeked around the big boulder and took a look, sure enough, there was the dim yellow reflection of lamp light showing at the one little window of the shack. Abe knew Balestine would be coming out soon to use the little one-holer outhouse about fifteen feet from the end of the cabin; it wasn't a minute later that the cabin door opened and Balestine appeared there, dressed in long-john flannel und#erwear, a pair of brown canvas pants with suspenders hanging at the sides; bare-footed he stepped carefully toward the outhouse, so as not to step on anything sharp.

Balestine wasn't a big man, he was round and stocky, but not fat, he kept himself well groomed. He had black, curly hair and a neatly trimmed full beard. His voice was deep and booming, it echoed through the woods as he sang some unknown folk song, as he moved along. There was a .45 caliber Schofield, jammed in the front of his britches for a left-hand pull. The heavy, long bladed, skinning knife he always carried, was not on him this morning.

Abe reached over and took hold of his Colt Lightning, slide action, rifle. He had bought it, at a steal of a deal, from a rancher who didn't like the action, however, Abe liked it because it could be rapid fired and it used the same cartridges as his Colt Army pistol. Abe had already chambered a round, so, he just waited for Balestine to go inside and get comfortable doing his business. He wasn't sure whether Balestine was standing or sitting, so, he aimed high enough to go over his head if he was upright. As he aimed high and started to squeeze the trigger, images haunted his mind; the killing of young Zander, the slaughter at the Burlington families ranch house, not to mention at least three saloon girls that he knew of.

Though, Abe had no positive proof yet, he knew for sure Salmon Balestine, had been hired secretly by the Stockmen's 'Protection League, down in the Credence area, or at the least by Masters McFerrin. He was pretty well convinced that he had been commissioned to discreetly rid the area of small settlement ranchers and farmers, trouble was they didn't realize Balestine didn't do anything discreetly. They were irritating the big cattle and sheep men operations by using barbed wire to fence off their homesteads. The big ranchers hated the wire, they wanted the land for open and free range, and many, just simply didn't like small homesteaders, nesting on free government land.

When Abe and a young sheriff's deputy went out to the Burlington families ranch, they found a horrible butchery. Little nine-year-old Tommy Burlington, dead. His father Tom, shot twice in the back. Thirteen-year-old Gloria and her mother had been tied with leather straps, partially stripped, and dishonored. It was the worst slaughter Abe had seen by any white man since the war. At the sight of it, the young sheriff's deputy, though pretty seasoned, lost his stomach, vomiting violently. Abe, thought

4

back to when he had buried the pretty saloon girl at May's place, and of the young man he buried on the road; both being killed by Salmon Balestine. Abe wondered what could possibly impel a man to such absolute wicked behavior. Abe, had never killed a man in cold blood, however, a madman like this was different.

He brought his aim down to where he knew it would send a bullet through Balestine's middle and started squeezing the trigger.

Before the rifle fired and sent a death dealing bullet into the door of the outhouse, an intense, sharp pain in the palm of his hand jolted him awake and into the reality of the moment. Abe struggled hard to suppress yelling out in pain. He quickly pulled his hand off the rock he had laid the fresh lit cheroot on. Abe pulled off his thin leather glove and looked at his palm, very red from what he tell by the dim morning light. Had it not been for the glove, it would surely have been blistered. Abe rubbed it gently with some moist earth to cool the sting, when the pain subsided somewhat, he tossed the cheroot and stone away. Then he peeked around the boulder and there was Balestine, headed toward the outhouse, pretty much like he had just pictured in his brief dream.

For real now, as Balestine stepped up and pulled the door shut, Abe aimed the rifle at the top of the shanty where he knew the round would surely go without hitting Balestine, and squeezed the trigger —BOOM. The crack of the rifle shot echoed through the woods and the slug ripped through the wood just above the door, sending splinters into the back of Balestine's head and neck. Abe, quickly worked the slide action of the Lightning, sending another round into the chamber. He took aim again, this time at the center of the door.

Balestine ducked his head and shouted from inside the little shanty, "WHAT DA HELL?" he yelled over his shoulder. "It is you…ain't it, Abie?"

"You're damned right it is, Balestine," Abe called down in reply.

"Am glad it is you ol' man. Another would have been killin' me."

"You listen here, you worthless ass. I will empty my rifle right through the middle of that door, unless, when you open it, you're facing out with that Schofield in the air above your head and your britches and clothes down around your ankles. Then you, just slowly turn around and drop that pistol down the hole. You understand? Do it quick, or that's where your useless, no count life, will end in about twenty seconds."

"I know you mean what you says, Abie. Sure, hate to lose this Scofield. Had it 'long time."

"Don't care. You're not gonna need it anymore. Do it, or die."

"Alright Abie, give me a minute to get myself finished."

Abe aimed and placed a second round through the wall, to left of the door, sending splinters into Balestine's lower backside. Abe shouted as he chambered the next round. "Times up," he shouted. He took aim at the center of the door.

"Yeah. I am doin' it." Balestine quickly striped his long-johns and the rest down to his ankles and turned with the Scofield above his head. He shoved the door open and stood there like Abe had instructed him.

"Now, slowly turn around, and drop that pistol down the hole."

He stood there in the doorway looking foolish, "How about, I just lay it down easy on the ground? Much a good gun to just throw…" Before Balestine got the words out, the answer came by way of a slug whizzing between his legs close to his private business.

"Damn Abie, you shore are an impatient some-a-gun." Balestine, complied with the instructions and turned, dropping the pistol down the hole.

"Now, keep those hands high, step out a few feet and pull your britches up."

"Yeah, sure Abie. You got me for now."

When Balestine was done pulling his clothes up, Abe motioned with his rifle and commanded, "Come on up here and join me, Balestine."

"Abie? Got no boots on."

"Get on up here, before, I put a big hole in your middle."

Balestine began to climb the hill to where Abe was. He hobbled up the hill slowly, carefully doing his best to avoid sharp rocks, twigs and sticks on the ground, which was starting to steam from the evaporating frost from the warming sun.

When he got there, Abe pointed with his rifle toward his horse, "Go on over to Nick there, and pull out the shackles in the saddlebags and fix them tight on your hands and ankles."

As Balestine got to the horse and touched

the saddlebags, Nick, swung his head around turning one ear forward and one back and snorted. Then he took a nip at him, causing him to step back out of his way.

"I don't think your horse like me so much, Abie."

"Him and me agree on a lot of things."

"I don't want to be in chains like no animal, Abie."

"You'll put them on yourself, or I'll use my rifle butt to hammer your ass to the ground, and then, I will put them on you. Besides, the way I figure it, you are, pretty much of an animal, Balestine."

"You have hard ways of persuasion, Abie. You and me are alike, you know? Just on different sides."

"No, I never kill anyone that don't deserve killin', and never for pleasure. You're a low-life murdering scum. Now, shut your mouth and get those irons on."

Balestine sat on the ground and snapped the iron shackles in place on his wrist and ankles. When he finished, he smiled, "What we got to do now, Abie?"

Abe walked over and twisted the keys back out of the shackles. "I'm takin' you down to Credence, where you'll stand trial. Then, I reckon they'll be hangin' you."

"Credence, is a long way, Abie. I be watching you sleeping."

"And, I'll always have a bullet with your name on it, ready."

Balestine smiled, "Looking forward to the trip, Abie."

"And, I'm looking forward to seein' you hang."

"How we going to get all that way down to Credence from here, Abie?"

"Well, let's you and me walk on down to the cabin there. We'll load up your wagon and hitch up those two horses of yours. I'll tie Nick behind, and we can head on down the road. Pretty simple, right."

"Sure. I got no ting but, little bacon, and one day maybe, coffee. That not enough to get us there."

2

Balestine liked to travel in a small wagon with two good horses to pull it. Abe figured that would be a good way for them to travel; they would follow the stage route on the main road. His plan was to put, Balestine, in the back of the wagon and shackle him to the side boards.

After securing Balestine in the wagon, Abe stepped out over the tailgate and to the ground. "We'll stop in Arland for supplies. First, I'm gonna make a stop at the little saloon down the road on the river and pick me up something."

"You pick up a little something for me too, Abie? I get you money."

"I wouldn't piss in your face, if your beard was on fire."

"Do not be like that, Abie."

"If you don't shut up, I'm gonna stuff a muddy rag in your face."

Balestine leaned back against the wagon sideboards and relaxed, he kept quite after that. He knew Abe had enough of his talking.

Abe went into the cabin, found Balestine's provisions, started a small fire in the little potbellied stove, put together what was left of the coffee, and fried half of the bacon. When everything was ready he found two tin cups, poured coffee and took them and the small skillet of bacon outside and shared them with Balestine.

After cleaning everything up and packing the wagon, Abe stripped Nick of his gear, put it all in the wagon and tied him to the back. He took his saddle blanket and gave Balestine some padding to set and lean on. He stowed Balestine's knife and other belongings under the wagon seat along with his rifle, then he climbed up into the seat.

"Wait," Balestine called.

"For what?"

"Where is my green bag?"

"Ya mean the bag with all the women's hair in it? Well, you see that light-colored stream of smoke comin' out of the stove pipe of the cabin there, I'd reckon that's what you're askin' me about."

Balestine's eyes narrowed and he gave Abe an icy glare. "You, no right to…" Abe slapped the reins and the horses jerked the wagon into forward motion, almost spilling Balestine over the tailgate as he cursed at Abe.

A few rugged miles up the road, on the

Grey Bull river, Abe reined the horses and wagon up in front of a saloon. He stepped down from the wagon, pulled the flask out of his vest pocket and emptied the contents into his mouth, wiped his mouth with his sleeve, put the stopper in it and slipped the flask back into his vest pocket. Abe walked to the back of the wagon and checked Balestine's shackles to make sure he was secured to the wagon. Then he went back to the front of the wagon, pulled his rifle from under the seat, worked the slide, chambering a new cartridge into place.

Abe went over, stepped up on the boardwalk of the saloon, walked to the double doors and entered in through the one on the right. Inside, he closed the door easy behind him. The warmth from a tall ornate wood stove took away the chill he felt from outside. Abe squinted his eyes in the dim light to look around the room. He could not make out much more than shadows at first. As his eyes adjusted and things started clearing up, he noticed a young woman in a dark green, lacy, low cut dress, that exposed most of her maturity, was seated at a small round table with two young cowboys. A barkeep was polishing glasses while talking to a man at the front end of the bar. A man sat at a table by himself and two men were standing, backs to the bar, with their heels hooked on the brass foot rail. Both, were looking curiously across the room, out the front window at the man shackled in the wagon.

"Ya some kind of a lawman?" asked the taller of the two.

"Shore, he is Clint. Don't ya see the badge," sneered the second man. This man had long stringy hair and a scantily grown mustache and chin whiskers. Both men took a stepped away from the bar, each had a six-shooter that hung low on their hip. Their pistols were of much better quality than the way they were dressed.

The one called Clint cautiously flipped the thong off the hammer of his pistol with his thumb. "Ya know, we don't cotton to lawmen much up here. Ain't that right, Beck?"

The one called Beck, tightened his jaw, his dark eyes narrowed. "Pretty much," he answered as he took a wide stance.

Abe took a long hard look into the man's eyes, "You, Beck Fuller?"

"Yep. You know of me, do ya?"

"As a matter of fact, I do. You killed a friend of mine down in Austin, Texas. And, I saw a wanted poster on you in Credence."

"Don't remember killin' no one down in Austin."

"Sure, you do, a fella named, Billy Pepper. You had a disagreement over a card game, you shot him in the belly, twice. Took three days for Pepper to die."

"Oh, that deal, Billy Pepper. Yeah, yeah. He was cheatin' and he drew down on me when I called him on it. It was self-defense."

"Not according to the witnesses. All he had on him was small folder knife."

"Yeah well, he tried to stab me with that pig sticker. Besides, a grand jury down in Credence, found it was self-defense."

"Is that a fact? How the hell did a grand jury in Credence, Wyoming make a ruling on a murder in Texas?"

"Had some witnesses myself, two of'm. They were there that night. Clint here, was one." Clint nodded and Beck smiled. "It was all…legal like."

"That's not the way I heard it. I suppose, Masters McFerrin and the Stockmen's Protection League, headed up that grand jury?"

Beck chuckled and looked over at Clint, who joined in the humor. "As a matter of fact, they did. So, what's that to you, lawman?"

Coolly Abe replied, "Like I said, Billy Pepper was a friend of mine, I knew his family well. He was no card cheat."

Beck steadied himself and gradually positioned his hand over the nickel plated .45, holstered at his side. "We-l-l, I tell ya…"

"Hey Beck," Clint interrupted, "He's got ol' Salmon Balestine out there in that wagon."

"What? —You sure?"

"Hell yeah. Look fer yerself."

Beck gave Abe a hard look, smiled wickedly. "Lawman, you got Salmon Balestine, out there, do ya?"

"I do. He's my prisoner."

Mean readiness filled Beck's eyes. "The Stockmen's Protection League has paid us to come up here and get him. We'll be taking him off yer hands. Thanks, for savin' us the trouble of trackin' him down."

Abe tightened his grip on the Lightning rifle in his right hand at his hip, "Nobody, takes a prisoner from me."

Beck and Clint both went for the pistols on their hips. Abe cracked off a shot and hit Beck full in the chest, fast as a half a blink, he worked the slide action of his rifle and put one in Clint's abdomen. Again, he quickly worked the action of the rifle as he noticed a sudden movement off to his right side. The lone cowboy at the table stood up and pulled his .45 six-shooter, before he could aim and fire, Abe put a bullet through his throat, right below his Adam's-apple, the man collapsed to the floor. As Abe turned back toward the first two men, Clint had struggled up on his knees, weakly he raised his pistol to take aim. Abe, in a flash worked the slide action once more and shot Clint in the forehead.

Again, Abe chambered a cartridge, eyes accustomed to the dim light now, they narrowed as he pointed the rifle around the room. He challenged, "Anyone else got any ideas of takin' my prisoner?"

The girl, had jumped up into the chair, peeing herself and buried her head in her dress, between her knees. One, of the cowboys that had been sitting with her was standing with his hands raised above his head to show he wasn't going to make any aggressive moves; the other just remained seated trying carefully not to move a muscle. The barkeep and the other fellow just stared at Abe, somewhat thunderstruck.

"Sorry about the mess," said Abe. "I just want a bottle of your best whiskey. Then, I'll be on my way and leave you to clean up. There is a two thousand-dollar reward for Beck down in, Texas. And, it would surprise me, if there wasn't something, somewhere, for Clint there either. Not anything I have an interest in, so, I'll leave that to you all to figure out."

The barkeep went to the shelf behind the bar and pick out a bottle and sat it on the bar. Abe walked over and looked at it. "Canadian, good choice. How much my friend?"

"I ain't no damned friend to you mister. For you whisky's five bucks."

"Fair enough," said Abe though he knew it wasn't. He kept the rifle in his right hand with his finger on the trigger, and with his left hand he reached inside his coat and pulled out a five-dollar gold piece from his vest pocket and tossed it on the bar, then he picked up the bottle. "Thanks," Abe smiled, "keep the rest." Then he carefully backed out of the saloon.

3

On his way to the front of the wagon Balestine asked, "What was all the shooting, Abie?"

Abe stowed the whisky and the Colt Lightning rifle under the seat. "Just a couple fellas that wanted to kill you, I'll explain later. Right now, we best get you out of here."

Balestine, started to asked another question as Abe slapped the reins, sending the wagon lurching forward, throwing him tumbling back against the tailgate, jarring him speechless and twisting the shackles tight around his arms. He struggled hard to upright himself and untwist the shackles, it wasn't easy, because of the wagon bouncing around. Finally, after a few minutes of hard struggle, he managed to get turned around in a position where he could ride more comfortable.

In Arland, as the wagon pulled up in front of the trading post, a light snow started falling. Balestine, peeked out from the blankets he had rolled himself up in to look around. He uncovered his head and called, "Hey Abie, be nice and get me ten or eight candy stick. I give you money, okay?"

Abe, heard him and totally ignored what he said. He climbed down from the wagon and as usual went back and made sure, Balestine was still secured to the side boards, in the shackles. He also helped him untangle the blankets, so he could cover himself proper. "Thank you, Abie. Hey, you get me candy sticks, please? Okay?"

Abe glared at him without saying a word, turned and walked into the trading post. Inside, two men were shopping around and there were five or six that sat and stood around a tall pot-bellied stove; it had an ornate silver colored pinnacle on top and one side of the stove had a dark red glowing spot; the men were warming themselves and talking. Three of the men, by the stove, younger fellas, went outside and started milling around the wagon, talking to Balestine. Abe kept a close eye on all of them as he started ordering some basic supplies from the store clerk; the last thing he ordered was a box of cartridges.

The store clerk packaged everything and talked to himself as he added it all up. Abe pulled out his poke and as he was counting what he had, he noticed a large jar of candy sticks sitting on the counter. He reached in the jar and pulled out two candy sticks and put them in his coat pocket. "Add these to my bill," he told the clerk.

"Oh- shore," the clerk smiled. Done figuring, the clerk told him the total of the sale, "That'll be eight dollars and fifty-two cents."

Abe paid, put his poke away and picked up the large package in both hands. Looking outside through a frosted window, he saw that Balestine was holding up his hands showing the shackles to the three men that were around the wagon. Balestine was talking and the three men were shaking their heads. He figured he better get outside and find out what Balestine was trying to work out with the three men. He put the package back on the counter and pulled his Colt, checked the load, spun the cylinder and put it back in place. He picked the package up again and walked to the door.

Abe went quickly to the front of the wagon and put the bundle down. The men were looking mean his way as he approached them. One spoke up, "Pretty extreme to leave a man shackled in the cold for just poaching, don't you think." The other men nodded in agreement. "We say," the man ordered, "let him go, or yer gonna have more trouble than yer gonna wanna deal with."

"So-o, that's the story he told you, is it?"

said Abe.

"Well, yeah," said one inquisitively. Another of the men reach across his belt to draw a .44 pistol.

In an instant, Abe had his Colt in the man's face. He said, "Trying to die for this murdering butcher would be a very large mistake.

"Let me tell you what he's really guilty of. Just since I have known of him, he has cut a beautiful young ladies throat after using her. And, then near three weeks ago, he slaughtered the Burlington family. You're probably not too fond of sod busters fencing in cattle, but this scum shot a nine-year-old boy in the head, a father in the back. Then, he defiled a young girl and her mother, and then, he butchered them both. Poaching? I don't think so. Now are you fellas sure you want to die here in the street for this animal?

"Now, put that pistol away and move on, before I have to shoot all three of you. I'm taking this man to hang."

The man who had been doing the talking, told his companion to put his pistol away. Then he turned and punched Balestine square in the face, nearly knocking him out and blooding his nose. "Sorry Marshall, good luck to ya." The three left quickly down the street.

Abe put away his Colt and reached in his pocket, pulled out the candy sticks showing them to Balestine, who's beard was all bloody from the punch in the face, but it didn't seem to bother him. "Abie, you a decent, thoughtful, man."

"Well, I was," said Abe, he pulled back his arm hurled the candy sticks down the street as far as he could. He then walked around the wagon and climbed up into the seat.

"Damn your hide, Abie. You som-a-gun, I cut your heart out for that; you and that cowboy what hit me."

Abe cocked his head listening and slapped the reins. As usual, the quick movement of the wagon, caught Balestine totally off guard, and tumbled him back against the tailgate, twisting his arms and the blankets in the shackles. He fought violently to untangle himself from the blankets and wrist shackles, cursing all the while. "Damned well, if I get my knife, I gonna slice hell outa you, som-a-bitch."

Abe paid no attention to his struggle because, he really at this point, didn't care.

Orin Vaughn

4

Abe, first came across Balestine, almost two years ago, down in Arizona Territory. Abe and a half bred Indian tracker named, Blood Bone, were after two young fellas who had kidnapped a banker's wife in Phoenix and killed her after not receiving a $5,000 ransom. The two were under the assumption the banker was rich, but he was just an employee who dressed well, with a large house supplied by his employer. The banker had little money himself and the people he worked for wasn't about to shell out anything, so the bank just turned it over to the US Federal Marshal's Service.

Blood Bone, was an exceptional tracker, however, Abe's Captain didn't want to put him on the payroll again, because, as he put it, he was a 'stinkin', one eyed, drunken bandit, Indian'.

It was said that Blood Bone, most just called him Bone, used to be a mountain man, a game hunter and when he slaughtered an animal he would cut out some bone and suck out the marrow, thus getting his face bloody. It was also told that, one day a few years back, while hunting buffalo, he was very drunk and he over loaded his rifle and it blew up in his face, putting out his eye. However, that didn't slow him down any; he learned to shoot and sight a rifle left handed and use his left eye to sight his six-shooter in his right hand very efficiently. He was however, easily blind-sided on his right; his hearing was exceptional, so it was difficult to sneak up on him. According to Blood Bone himself, he was Apache. Some say his mother was Apache and his father was a black trapper. Bone bragged that, he once rode with Geronimo. No one knew for sure, but it would certainly fit his personality. Most, didn't like him, like the Captain. Abe and he got along fine, even drank together a number of times. Abe was probably the only one who trusted him. Bone showed appreciation of their friendship by being loyal to the point of death.

Abe told the Captain, Bone was the best tracker he had ever known, besides that, he would work for thirty-five-cents a day and a 5th of cheap whisky a week. So, with a little talking the Captain gave in, mostly because, he wanted those dumb kidnappers caught.

Three days later, Abe and Bone found the two of them camped south of Benson in a wash, just seven or eight miles from Tombstone. Abe gave the two every opportunely to give up and surrender peacefully. They didn't want any part of that and decided to shoot their way out of the situation. The young men put up an impressive fight, but ended up shot all to pieces; one suffered five major bullet wounds and still took almost a half hour to die afterward. The other was hit a number of times and ended up being killed by a bullet in the head and died instantly. Bone had a bullet hole through the top of his hat, which he just smiled at, other than that they suffered no damages.

After Abe and Bone brought the two kidnapper's bodies in, the appreciative Captain thanked them, and dismissed Bone after paying him, he even gave him a little bonus. Then he said to Abe, "I'll be sending you up to the Credence, Wyoming area to help out the Deputy County Sheriff, with some trouble between cattlemen and farmers."

Abe didn't seem to have a problem with that, he usually took on whatever he was assigned. "Never been that far north. Might be a nice change."

"Don't get too excited," said the Captain. "The weather up there can get pretty damn brutal in the winter. Not shy on snow neither, might even have some before you get there."

"Been in bad weather before."

After getting the details of his assignment and who to contact in Wyoming, Abe left the office. Bone was waiting outside by his horse. "Where might you be going now?"

"Way north, Wyoming. Gonna stop and visit an old friend first. I ain't seen her in a long time, she's just north of Phoenix a bit. Mavis May's Place, ever been there?"

"Heard of it."

"You wanna join me?"

"Got nothing better to do right now. So, sure, why not."

Mavis May's Place was usually very lively, however today, there were only three horses outside on the rail; two of the horses were in definite need of care. Abe and Bone dismounted cautiously, sensing something wasn't right, it was an uneasy feeling that both these men of experience felt. Abe checked the load in his Colt Army, then he pulled his rifle, the Colt Lightning, from the scabbard on Nick's saddle. He tied Nick loose and whispered in his ear, "Be ready Nick...don't know what's comin' up." Nick's ears turned back listening to him as if he knew exactly what he was saying. Abe then worked the slide action of his rifle chambering a round.

Bone, checked the loads in his Remington cartridge conversion, and the two men, ready for anything, stepped up on the porch of Mavis May's Place. Abe and Bone crossed the wooden planked floor stepping slowly, but the old wood floor cricked with almost every step they took. Abe pushed through the swinging doors carefully with his rifle ready for action.

Once inside, he saw Mavis May, a black cowboy, a black barmaid and Big Dan the bartender, who was sitting in an armchair with his chest and shoulder wrapped with bandages. Close to the middle of his chest was a four to five-inch spot of blood-soaked bandage. The four seemed to be in a serious conversation as Abe and Bone approached, while checking every dark corner for movement, ready for action as they worked their way around tables and chairs to join the four at the end of the bar. Mavis May, suddenly caught sight of Abe and her face lit up. She smiled wide and went directly to Abe's welcoming arms and kissed him passionately on the mouth. She hugged him tight, looked at him very seriously and said, "I am so glad you're here. So, very glad."

"What's going on May? What happened to Big Dan?"

"The last four days have been just holy hell around here, I swear."

5

Abe and Mavis May, went back a way. She had been a saloon girl in Dallas, Texas when Abe first met her. Being a beautiful black woman, some cowboys wanted to abuse and treat her harsh. One night, two cowhands, feeling their liquor decided they were going to take her on top of a table right there in the middle of the saloon, while everyone watched. A crowd of six or eight cowboys were cheering the two of them on. May, what Abe always called her, was holding her own to resist when another cowboy decided to join in. Abe had enough of this, he went over and cracked one of the offenders up side of his head with his pistol, then he pointed it at the crowd and said, "Parties over here, fellas. Go find some fun somewhere else."

"Just who the hell do you think you are tryin' to tell us what to do?" said a rugged looking cowboy in the crowd.

Abe cocked the Colt and said, "Abe Wallace, is the name. And, since you spoke up first, you're the first one I'm gonna put a large hole in, unless you all don't just move on."

"You can't shoot us all mister before, we

get'cha," challenged the rugged cowboy.

"You're right. But, you'll die first," he pointed the pistol at another cowboy, "And, then you, and maybe I'll be able to take you. Could even get another one or two. This ain't my first dance. Now, make your move, or get."

"Let's go find somewhere else to drink," said the rugged cowboy as he turned to leave, the others followed. On their way, a couple of them helped the one Abe cracked in the head, get up off the floor and stagger away. Thus started a very close relationship.

Now with Abe there, May started explaining the events of the last four days at her place. "Four days ago," she started, "these three fellas came in here and started drinking and bein' friendly with four of my girls. After about an hour, they all went upstairs. An hour or so after that, one of the fellas came down. A short sturdy fella with a beard…well-groomed fella he was. Anyway, he came down by himself, none of the girls was with him. Didn't think much of it; he paid his bar tab, even gave extra, 'for the girl' he said. Pretty Patty, everyone called her, she had long blond hair. Then he bought a bottle of good whiskey and rode out in a small buckboard with high sides.

All well and good, or so I thought. That poor girl, she was so pretty."

"The other two were upstairs with my three girls over two hours, just about the time I was gonna send Big Dan up, Percy, came down and said, 'The guy's upstairs are wantin' some food'.

"She seemed a little uncomfortable. But, she's an experience gal. So, Big Dan fixed up some food and Percy took it up."

"Do you know these fellas?" asked Abe. Blood Bone was quiet, he just listened. "Have you ever seen any of them before? What do they look like?"

"No, never. I don't believe they're from around here. There's a tall red headed man with a full beard, says he's from Texas, calls himself, Rowdy Red Hamond. The last fella is not much more than a kid, in fact, he referred to himself as the Arkansas Kid."

"Heard of Rowdy Red Hamond," said Abe. "Drinks hard, lives hard, robs banks and trains. He's a dangerous man. Never heard of no Arkansas Kid, though."

Abe looked over at Bone, he shook his head.

"Go on, what happened May?"

"Well, they spent the night. It was pretty noisy up there most of the night. In the morning, I figgered it was time to break things up and settle accounts. I sent Big Dan upstairs to let those two know we needed to get on with our business, and resolve and close up our business with them.

So, Dan went up and banged on the door where Rowdy Red was and told them through the door that, 'it was time to settle up their account'. The answer he got was, Rowdy Red sent two shots through the door, one hitting Big Dan in the chest. He fell to the floor, the door opened and Rowdy Red came out, half-dressed and a pistol in each hand. He kicked Dan to the stairway and halfway down the stairs, and then, he pushed him the rest of the way down with his foot. Before, I could get my hands on the shotgun from behind the bar, he shot at one of my customers, there were about fifteen people down stairs. 'Clear out all'a ya, or al'm gonna put y'all to rest in short order. I mean it now. I ain't kiddin''. Then he shot a hole in the middle of a poker table where four fellas were playin' and sent them a runnin'. The place cleared out and me, Dan and Jealous Jane here, was the only ones left in the place.

"We took care of Dan as best we could and made him comfortable, that was two days ago. I got to wonderin' why Patty hadn't come down, so I went up to see. I went upstairs with the shot-gun ready. I was horrified when I opened the door. Pretty Patty was face down on the bed, dressed, hands tied behind her back by leather straps; her throat was cut and her hair nearly all cut off. I was so shocked, I just came down stairs. Every once'n a while Percy comes down and gets some food and liquor for them. She told us that Rowdy Red said, that if anybody comes up the stairs besides her, he will kill Sheri Kay and Moanie, the other two girls, and then kill anyone else in the saloon. Well, that's the sad story, Abe. What can we do? I don't want my girls killed."

6

"**W**ell," said Abe, "let's get this business settled. Bone, you and May stay down here, ready to take care of anyone who comes down those stairs except me or yer girls. Get the shotgun, May. What's your name cowboy?"

"Carl Washington, sir."

"Okay Carl," said Abe, "you and me will go upstairs and deal with those two upstairs. Let's go."

"Naw, hell no," said Carl.

"You don't look like a man that's subject to cowardice, Carl?"

"I ain't sir, but, I don't wanna hang for killin' no white man neither. I just came here to visit my sister, Jane."

"Well, here's what I'll do, Carl. I'm a US Federal Marshal, I'll deputize you and it will all be good and proper. As a deputy, you'll have the authority to do what I tell you. How's that suit you?"

"A deputy huh? All legal and good you say?"

"Yep."

"All right," said Carl confidently.

Abe told Carl to raise his right hand and then he mumbled some official sounding words and said, "Alright, do you solemnly swear to uphold the law in this undertaking, if so, say I do."

"Yes sir, I do."

"Alright then. Let's go upstairs and get this business done.

"Which rooms are they in, May?"

"There's three rooms up there. Poor Patty's in the first room right at the top of the stairs, the Kid is in the first room to the left with Percy. Big Red is in the last room with Sheri Kay and Moanie. Oh, better let you know, there's a door that connects the two rooms."

"You're Jane, Carl's sister I reckon?" Abe said to the black barmaid.

"Yes, I am," she replied.

"Know how to shoot a gun?"

"I used to hunt with a rifle when I was a kid, back in Alabama, squirrels and such."

"Ever shot anyone?"

"Nope, but shootin' any of those animals upstairs would be no harder than shootin' squirrels back in Alabama."

"Good," Abe handed Jane the Lightning that he had leaned against the bar. "It's ready now, and if you need to shoot more, you just simply slide this back toward yourself and you're ready to go again. Got it Jane?"

"Sure enough."

"Alright. Let's go, Carl. Bone, you know what to do." Bone nodded. May got the 10-gauge and moved closer to the staircase as Abe and Carl stepped lightly up the stairs, Abe in the lead.

Mavis May, was a very successful saloon girl back in Texas. She was so trusted by the owner, that she got to manage the Texas Rose Saloon. She saved and went without, until she had enough money to buy her own business. She bought the Wild Cat Saloon, frequented by ranchers, a couple gamblers, and a lot of local cowboys; fixed up the place, hired some girls and became a very successful business woman. This was the first serious trouble she had in the three years since she opened the place.

When Abe and Carl reached the top of the stairs, they both pulled their pistols and cocked them. Abe motioned for Carl and when he was close enough, he whispered, "Let's kick in the doors at the same time. Go to the door, and when we get in position I'll count, one, two, three and we'll do it together. Don't be afraid to kill him and don't take any chances."

They each got in position, Abe at the door

where Rowdy Red was, he looked at Carl and silently mouthed the numbers, one, two—three.

Both doors flew open at the same time as planned. Abe surprised Hamond, who was standing naked in front of a dresser with a pitcher and wash bowl on top, looking in the mirror. The large man moved fast and went around to the end of the dresser, grabbed a pistol from his holster outfit that was hanging on the dresser mirror. Abe got off a shot that winged Hamond in the right arm, just a flesh wound, as he disappeared through the door between the rooms. Abe quickly went to the doorway, as he did he told the girls who were in the bed to, "stay put". When he got to the doorway he saw Hamond just as he was about to fire on Carl who had his pistol trained on the young lad in the bed with Percy. Abe leveled his Colt and shot him in the head, right behind the ear, from about three feet away; blood spattered on the bed that Percy was in with the young man, the so-called Arkansas Kid, who was in a half-seated position, with hands held as high as he could get them, leaning against the metal head frame. "I *give* up," he called out. "I ain't got no gun in this bed, I swear."

"Get out'a that bed boy," ordered Abe.

"But sir, I have no clothes on."

"If you wanna keep living, get your ass up, right now."

"Okay, just don't shoot me, please."

The young man, not much more than a kid, got up pulling the blanket with him to cover his nakedness, exposing Percy's bare breast. "Let go of that blanket before I shoot your rotten ass."

The boy dropped the blanket and Percy pulled up the slack, covering herself.

"Now kid, you stand there and look her in the eye and apologize to the lady for causing her grief, or you won't live to see the sun go down today."

The young man looked at Percy in a shameful manner and said, "I am real sorry Miss Percy, for the trouble I caused you, in the last few days mam."

"Now go over and apologize to the other two ladies in the next room."

"Well, I never had..." the kid was motivated to shut up and do what he was told by Abe's hard expression and the wave of his pistol.

The kid, all red faced and ashamed, went in to the next room with Abe right behind him. "I better believe you're sincere or it ain't gonna be good."

With his head down, and his hands covering himself as best he could, he meekly apologized to the two women still in the bed, much in the same words as he had Percy. The two women smiled and kind of giggled.

"You get your butt down stairs now, boy," said Abe. The kid started to return to the other bedroom, but Abe stopped him. "Just where the hell do you think you're going there?"

"To get my clothes, sir."

"No, you're not. I said, get your naked butt down stairs. Get going."

The kid started to say something, but didn't. He realized that Abe meant what he said. There would be no conversation on the matter. The kid started for the stairs still trying to keep himself covered with his hands. Abe was right behind him and Carl behind Abe. About halfway down, Abe shoved the kid with his foot the rest of the way down the stairs and he tumbled hard to the bottom, ending up on the floor at the foot of the stairs sprawled out on his back, totally exposed.

May, Bone and Jealous Jane, with their guns ready, just stared at him as if he was some kind of circus act.

Then he struggled to set up, moaning as he

got himself upright to a standing position, then he remembered he was naked and quickly covered himself.

Mean eyed, Abe asked, "One of those nags outside belong to you, boy?"

"Yes sir," he replied.

"You get on'm and ride out of here. If I ever see your face again, I'll shoot you on the spot."

"But sir, I'm naked. I need my clothes."

"Be happy I am letting you get out of here with your skin. Now, get going, I'm tired of being nice to you."

The young man was quite befuddled as he moved toward the door, still making an effort to keep himself covered with his hands. Bone, chuckled low, and Carl just plain laughed out loud. May said, "Let the boy get his clothes, for Pete-sake."

"Nope. He's got to learn a lesson from this. Hey kid," Abe called.

The young man turned sideways, trying not to expose himself as best he could, and replied sheepishly, "Yes sir."

"You learn a lesson from this. You best make a better choice of friends from now on."

"Yes sir, I will."

"Kid, one more thing before you leave. What's the name of the fella that was with you all, the one who left here that first day?"

"Said his name was Salmon Balestine, talked kinda funny. He told me and Red one night, while we's sittin' round the campfire, that he had killed a young whore in Tucson, and cut off her beautiful hair. Said, he liked women's pretty long hair. Don't know nothin' more about him. He just joined up with us in Tucson, said we could outlaw together. He was headed for Colorada and, so was we." Then he quickly pushed through the saloon doors and went to his horse and pulled out an old, well-worn, dusty poncho from his saddlebag, threw it over his head, then mounted his horse and disappeared up the road.

7

Abe, May and the rest of the group downstairs, gathered at the bar. Big Dan was nearby, leaning back in a chair with his feet propped up on top of a table. Abe went over to Dan, "You mind if I take a look?"

"I reckon not, sure, go ahead."

Abe carefully undone the dressings covering Dan's wound. He wanted to see how serious Dan's gunshot wound was; the nearest doctor was near twenty miles away and probably would be hard to find. May went behind the bar, sat glasses on the bar for everyone and poured a double shot of good Canadian Whisky in each one.

"Me too," called Dan.

The wound had been cleaned and dressed very properly; Abe observed that Dan had been rather fortunate that the bullet had passed all the way through without hitting anything vital. Dan was in good health and if the wound was kept clean and the dressings changed regularly, there was no reason he wouldn't heal up pretty fast. Abe informed everyone what he thought about it, as Jealous Jane, brought their drinks over. "He's gonna heal up fine. Just keep the wound clean and new dressings on it regular. You'll do alright Dan," Abe assured as he put a firm hand on Dan's other shoulder. Dan nodded, raised his glass to everyone, then downed it.

All the men, pretty well threw theirs down in one big swallow, while the women, sipped theirs in three or four drinks.

Abe joined the group at the bar. "Something I'm wondering about. Why didn't you send for the Sheriff?"

May took a deep breath, "Humph— We-l-l, he nor any of his deputies, will come out here."

"Why, the hell not?"

"It's, kind of complicated. You see, the Sheriff wants me to pay taxes and get licenses for my girls. And, he also wants my girls to indulge him and his deputies whenever they want. I told him that that wasn't gonna happen. I ain't payin' no taxes, and I sure in hell ain't given my girls for nothin'."

"Well, that's extortion. I'll look into that and see what can be done."

"No, please don't bother. I like it, just the way it is. Don't need no law noisin' around my place anyway."

"I don't like it, but I will abide by your wishes. Normally, I would be headed out after this, what his name, Salmon Balestine, but I want a good night's rest in a bed— how about you Bone?"

"Yes," he looked at May, holding up his glass. "A-nother?"

"Shore, anyone else?"

All three men nodded their heads in response. So, she poured another round for them. As she poured Abe's glass, she looked deeply into his steel gray eyes; May was a bit younger than Abe, she had always cared for him, she was still quite a looker, her medium brown eyes gleamed. "Well, we can shore accommodate you fellas for tonight," she said. "I'll go up and see how my girls are doin' and help straighten up the bedrooms.

"What do you want done with that dead hombre upstairs? Oh, and, I got to see that Pretty Patty, is laid to rest proper."

"Me, and the boys here, will see to it," replied Abe. "We'll help you with your girl first though."

"I appreciate it. There's some tools out back in a little shed. I'm sure you'll find a shovel there." May had held up pretty good, but now her eyes welled up, and she fought back her emotions; nonetheless a single tear escaped and slowly drifted down her cheek, "If...if, you would, bury Patty out back, by the polo verde and mesquite trees, among the rock garden and cactus. She always said that if anything ever happened to her she wanted to be buried in a peaceful place like that."

Abe went out and started digging the graves, while Carl and Bone brought the bodies down wrapped in sheets. After the grave was dug and she was placed in it, the dirt thrown over it, they all stood around Patty's grave. May, bowed her head and said, "Lord, she's in your hands now."

There was a lot less care taken with Rowdy Red's burial, out a way, just a few feet from the foot of a dead yucca and a patch of Cholla cactus in the desert, the men tossed him in the hole, covered it and walked away.

Bone was up before dawn, earlier than anyone else, despite the fact he had polished off most of a bottle of whisky before going to sleep. He was behind the saloon setting on his heals watching the sun come up in all of its Arizona brilliance; he enjoyed solitude, socializing wasn't something he cared for. He liked Abe, because he didn't push anything on him, just told him what needed to be done, so he could do it. As far as he was concerned, Abe was his only real friend, and all he cared to have.

The morning sun was pleasantly warming the day. Abe and May were sitting drinking coffee on the boardwalk in front of the saloon after breakfast; Bone came around from the back and joined them. He slid down the front of the saloon, near where they were, sitting down with his legs crossed. He leaned over and handed May a little round metal container, "Put some of this on Big Dan's wound, two times a day. It will help it heal faster and prevent infection."

She nodded to his request with an appreciative expression, then turned to Abe, "Abe, where's the wind takin' you now?" She knew Abe didn't stay in one place too long, it just wasn't in his nature.

"We-l-l, I figured me and Bone would try to catch up with this, Balestine fella, before he gets to Colorado. Then, I'll be headed for Wyoming. I have been assigned to help with some trouble up there."

Bone looked at Abe curiously, "Whisky?"

"Sure, Bone."

"Captain will not pay," Bone said shaking his head.

"If not Bone, I'll pay you."

49

"Just whisky then."

Abe looked over at May and smiled. "Bone's a man of few words."

She smiled back, "Kinda...gathered that." Abe had just taken the last drink of his coffee, when he saw May smiling and looking cross-eyed at him, he choked a laugh and spewed it back in the cup, they all laughed.

"Good women for you," said Bone.

"What do you know about women?" asked Abe.

"I have known plenty women. If they can make you laugh, they are good for you." They all smiled and laughed again.

"There's bacon, eggs and coffee, Bone," May gestured with her head toward inside. "Dan will show you."

"Good— thank you," Bone got up and went inside.

A little later, about ten-o'clock, they were all standing on the porch of the saloon, saying their good-byes. Bone stepped off the boardwalk and went to his horse and threw himself up in the saddle in one leap. May, handed Abe a tall bottle of Canadian whisky and a bag of hardtack and beans. Then she pulled Abe in close and kissed him passionately. With her face so close that she move his mustache with her lips when she talked, "Please, come back to me."

"I'll do my best. But, you never know what lays ahead. Well, bye May."

"Take care. You too, Bone."

Bone tipped the front brim of his hat with his thumb and forefinger. Abe waved to everyone as they turned and rode off. May watched somberly until they disappeared into specks on the road.

Abe Wallace: U.S. Federal Marshal

8

Bone stopped his horse, he looked back down the road. Abe held up beside him, Bone looked over at him. "I know, Nick's been tellin' me with his ears for the last couple of miles." Bone jumped off his horse and handed the reins to Abe. Then he disappeared running into the trees and bush. They were just a few miles from crossing into Colorado.

It hadn't been ten minutes when Bone came up the road riding a horse with a six-shooter pointed at the back of the kid from the saloon walking in front of him.

"Well now, look here— if it ain't the Arkansas Kid. I see you found some pants and shoes."

"And a pistol," said Bone waving an old, well-worn, Merwin-Hulbert, .45 revolver in the air. "Though, I am not so sure it will fire without blowing up in your face."

Abe adjusted himself in the saddle and stared down at the young man. "Just what are you up to, Kid? Was you planning on dolin' out some vengeance, youngster?"

"No-o sir, nothin' like that. You said, I should find better friends. So, that's why I wanted to catch up with you fellas."

"Well sonny, I'm a US Federal Marshal. And, Bone there, is my deputy. Don't need any young fool tag-a-longs. I'm afraid you'll have to find, better friends, your own age somewhere else."

"No sir— I mean, that Balestine fella, he killed that pretty women back at the saloon, didn't he?"

"Yep, he sure the hell did. And, we're gonna track him down and see him hanged."

"Well, I didn't like him no-how. I wanna be in on his capture and see him hanged. I won't be no trouble to ya. I just wanna be part of somethin' good for a change. You fellas 're better'n anyone I kin think of for friends. A'lm a good cook and I'd be willin' to do anything I can for y'all, if ya just let me be some part of bringin' that mean man to justice."

"He is more than a mean man, I am a mean man," said Bone, "he is a rabid animal, a devil and needs to be put down."

"True, Bone. Well, I am tired of eatin' hard-tack, beans and the desert rats that Bone's been feedin' me." Bone gave Abe a hard look.

"Ya mean, I kin go with y'all?"

"We'll give it a try, a least for a while," said Abe.

"Ya won't be so'ry. I'll do anythin' y'all tell

me."

There was something about this kid that Abe liked, "Alright then. Stay close, it'll be dark by the time we cross into Colorado. Then we'll see how good you can cook, kid. That is, if Bone will kill us some game."

"Sure, I will be happy to kill you another desert rat, Abe."

"Aw, come on now Bone. You know I was just funnin'."

Bone stiffened his bottom lip, "I was not."

The evening sun cast intense strikes of red, yellow-orange and purple across the western sky; all three men admired the spectacular vista. The sun disappeared behind distant mountains, yet it still ignited the sky with magnificent colorful flowing washes. Abe, rode over to a stand of trees that were half enclosed by a large rock formation and dismounted. "Let's camp here for tonight."

Bone nodded and the kid replied, "Shore, I'll start gatherin' wood fer a fire."

Bone pulled his Winchester out of the scabbard on his saddle and levered a round into place with a sharp metallic sound. "I will see if I can scare up a grouse or something."

Abe nodded and smiled, "Maybe two, Bone.

The boy needs to put some meat on his bones. He looks pretty damned hungry."

An hour later the kid had two birds roasting on a wooden spit he had made with green sticks. He stood up and pulled his neckerchief from around his neck and wrapped it around his hand. He went to the fire and grabbed the handle of the coffee pot and picked it up. Then he filled the other men's cups, then his own. He replaced the pot and turned the birds on the spit. "The fowls should be ready in just a bit. I wanna thank you fellas fer letting me come along."

Abe acknowledged his appreciative comment with a smile and a nod. "Sure kid. I wanna ask you a couple questions."

"Shore thing. Go right ahead."

"You don't seem the sort to be partnering up with the likes of those two back at the saloon. So, what's the deal?"

"Well sir…"

"Don't keep calling me, sir. My names Abe— Abe Wallace. And, I don't wanna keep calling you kid, so, what is your name?"

"My name is, Zander Bartlett. Big Red was my uncle on my maw's side. My paw died when him and Big Red were tryin' to rob a stage back a couple years ago. Maw died of consumption a month or so back, and Big Red took me on with him. Taught me how to handle a six-shooter. Said, he had just robbed a couple banks and we would take it easy fer awhile. Then, he was gonna learn me how to rob banks and stage coaches. He told me from then on, I was gonna be, the Arkansas Kid."

"You, robbed anybody yet?"

"No sir… I mean Abe."

"Just how old are you, Zan?"

"I'll be seventeen my next birt'day."

"When is that?" asked Bone.

"Next month sometime. Never knew what day I's born. Oh-h, the fowl is cooked. We should eat'm now." Zander removed the birds from the spit and placed them on a tin plate. Bone offered his hunting knife to cut the meat off the bone. After carving up the birds, he divided the meat up on two other plates in equal portions; he spooned out some beans on all three plates from a can he had heating close by the fire on a rock.

They started eating and when they were finished, Zander cleaned and put everything away, except for the coffee pot. Abe took a sip from his cup and started his questioning again. "Where'd you get the pants, shoes and gun?"

"I had twelve dollars in my saddle bags. A few miles up the road from the saloon, I was lucky enough to meet up with a panhandler driving a big wagon. He had everything you could imagine in that ther wagon. I bought the clothes fer three dollars, the pistol and a dozen cartridges fer the rest of my money. I asked the panhandler fer a free cartridge to make shore the pistol would fire. He said I was a good customer and gave me one; I fired it, and it worked fine."

"Well Bone, I think we can give Zan here back his pistol, don't you?"

Bone was laying against his saddle and said nothing. He reached over to his saddlebags and pulled out the pistol. Then he held it out to Zan by the barrel.

He walked over to Bone and took it and stuffed it in the front of his britches and said, "Thanks Bone."

"Do not get any ideas about using it against me or Abe."

"No— Never, would I even think of that."

"Good," said Bone.

"Bone's not a very trusting soul," Abe snickered.

"I think I kin understand that," replied Zan.

Bone leaned back on his saddle and pulled

his Indian blanket up to his shoulders, "Better sleep. Want to be rested when we catch up with that wagon in the morning."

Zan gave a hard-curious glance at each man, "What wagon are ya talkin' about?"

"Why, Balestine's wagon of course," replied Abe. "We've been followin' his wheel tracks ever since we left the saloon, you know."

"Oh...right. Dent know we were that close to him. Well, good night...Abe, Bone."

"Zan, we got to be cautious, this man will kill if cornered, without a second thought. You just listen to anything me or Bone tell you, understand?"

"Yes sir...uh Abe."

Abe Wallace: U.S. Federal Marshal

9

Zan woke up to the smell of bacon cooking. When he opened his eyes, he saw Bone pulling a skillet off the fire and Abe was saddling the horses and getting the gear ready.

"Sorry fellas, I dent wake up and do my part this mornin'."

"Good," said Bone. "Eat some bacon and then put out the fire. Leave some bacon for us."

"Shore thing."

Abe settled into the saddle. "How long before we catch up?"

"Not sure. Depends on how long he camped last night. Usually, he stops for six to eight hours. I am thinking maybe three or four hours. We do not want to come up on him too fast. If he knows we are coming, he might ambush us."

It had been almost four hours since they had broken camp when they came up on Balestine's wagon. It was sitting in the middle of the road, the horses pulling the wagon were tied down to a block while eating from feed bags attached to their bridles.

Bone's jaw tightened and his dark eyes

narrowed, "This does not feel right."

Zan stopped behind the two of them and twisted his neck around looking everywhere, "Maybe he's makin' a nature call."

Bone dismounted to examine the wagon and the area around it. He walked around the wagon looking for some sign of where Balestine might have gone.

"Stay put Zan," Abe nudged Nick forward. He eased up beside the wagon and started to dismount; suddenly Balestine broke out of the bushes and jumped up into the saddle behind Zan. Abe, taken by surprise, almost fell as his feet hit the ground. He quickly recovered his balance and drew his pistol. Bone was in front of the wagon with his pistol drawn and aimed. Balestine however, had a large hunting knife to the boy's throat. If Bone or Abe would have had a clear shot, without harming the boy, they would have taken it. Balestine kept himself well concealed behind Zan.

"You men, throw 'em guns in the dirt or I will certainly cut this lad."

Abe complied, but Bone kept a steady aim. Balestine drew the knife slowly, but lightly, across Zan's neck an inch or so. The boy wrinkled his face from the sting as a thin red line of blood formed and ran down his neck, attesting to the knifes razor sharp edge.

Abe glared at his partner, "BONE." Bone glared back and tossed his pistol to the side on the ground reluctantly.

"You men stand straight and still." Balestine looked over Zander's shoulder at his face. "Well lad, who are these fine fellows who you have buddied up with now?"

Zan's fearful, yet bold voice answered, "The tall one is Abe Wallace, a United States Federal Marshal and the other is his deputy. We're here to see that ya hang fer killin' that pretty lady back at the saloon."

"Is that so, see me hang, huh? You brought lawmen down on me? After we were outlawing together." Balestine, shook his head contemptibly. "You, Marshal man, get a few rawhide strips out of wagon and tie up your deputy. Does a good job now, or, I kill this lad here, understand? Hands 'n feet, both."

Grudgingly, Abe did as he was told. As he started, he whispered to Bone, "Take a deep breath and hold it while I tie you." Bone's dark repulsive eyes said he understood. When he was done and Bone let out the breath, the straps loosened ever so little. Bone was sitting on the ground about three feet from the wagon.

"You do a good job, Abie. Now, go sit on that big rock over there."

Abe did as he was told and followed instruction. As he was in the course of setting down, Balestine pulled the big knife deeply across Zander's throat. Blood gushed from his neck, his wide open blue eyes filled with horror as he gurgled blood out of his mouth; Abe stood up and started to run for Balestine, "You rotten, lousy, son-of-a bitch. I *will* kill you."

Before, Abe got three or four steps, Balestine put the knife in his left hand and as he pushed the boy off to the side of the horse, he drew the boy's pistol out of his belt. The limp body of Zan hit the ground with a lifeless thud and rolled to the side of the road. Abe was about four feet away from Balestine when he cocked the pistol and aimed it at Abe's face. "I'm pretty good shot, I blow you face off, easy."

It took every bit of rational thinking that Abe could muster to stop himself before Balestine carried out his threat. "You're a rotten son-of-a-bitch," Abe gnashed his teeth, glaring white hot anger out of his steel grey eyes, "I *will* surely kill you, if I ever get the chance."

"You might get that chance sometime, but

not this day, Abie."

"Why did you do that, he was just a boy?"

"He brought down the law on me, he was su'pose to be a partner."

"Well, what are you gonna do now?"

"I'm gonna tie you up, and leave the two of you for wild animal food. The smell'a the boy will get'm comin' in."

Balestine swung his leg over the horse's head and slide to the ground, all the time keeping the pistol aimed at Abe. He directed Abe with the pistol toward where Bone was sitting on the ground.

"You just keep yourself standin' up ere and go on over to the wagon an' get some more rawhide straps."

"You expecting me to tie myself up?"

"Yeah, kinda, there's a real long strap in nere. Pull it out an' tie one end to the top of that wagon wheel."

"This what you want?" Abe, looped the end of the strap around the wheel and secured it. It was about thirty feet long.

"Yeah, that's real good. Take it an' walk it to the end." Abe did what Balestine told him.

When he got to the end Balestine said, "Okay, good. Now, slip it through the front of your belt and tie it real good."

"Wh-at?"

"Come, Abie. Ya know what I want."

Abe poked it through the front of his belt. "This what you want?"

"That is good." Balestine motioned with the pistol. "Now, back and tighten up that strap. Yeah, that is it. Abie, put your arms at your sides and spin like a happy dance girl. Remember keep that strap tight; come all the way to wagon." Abe started turning around and around, rolling himself loosely up in the strap. Balestine stepped over to where Bone sat and back handed him on the cheek with the pistol, nearly knocking him out. "Stop. Damn it Abie. You keep that damn strap tight or I will scalp this dog-gone Ingun. Roll back and start again."

"Alright," roared Abe mean faced. "Damn you Balestine."

When Abe got to the wagon Balestine untied the end of the strapping and secured it behind Abe's back. "Good, Abie. Much more better." Abe could hardly move his arms. "Now Abie, go sit down by your Injun buddy." Unable to balance himself without the use of his arms, Abe plopped down beside Bone, hitting the ground pretty hard, jarring his breath a bit. When Abe secured himself upright, he looked at Bone and noticed blood running down from a gash on his cheek.

"Good, Abie," said Balestine, "I gonna tie your feet now." After he finished, he went to the back of the wagon and put on a pair of leather gloves, went over to the side of the road, bent down and picked up something from the ground. "Got no cocka-burs round this country," he grumbled. He held up a couple of very small cactus, "I think this'll do it." He went to the horse that Zander had been riding, he lifted the horses tail and placed the tiny cactus way back under the tail and slapped the animal on the butt firmly. The animal kicked high, almost hitting him with his rear hoof, the horse whistled piercingly and ran for his life. Then he did the same with Bone's horse, with much the same reaction. However, when he headed Nick's way, he reared up, screeched, and ran away in the same direction of the others horses.

"Well, smart horse," said Balestine. He climbed up into his wagon and tossed the Merwin-Hulbert .45 into the bushes. "Don't need that, I got a good gun." He patted the Scofield in his belt. "Well you fellows, keep your selves good…Hee-hee."

"I promise, I'll hunt you down and settle

the score, Balestine," roared Abe.

"Like, I said...mebee. But, not this day." Balestine slapped the reins and the wagon jerked in to motion, it quickly disappeared up the road.

Orin Vaughn

10

"You got any wiggle around room in those straps, Bone?"

"Yeah some, but I do not think I will be able to get out of them soon, if ever. I will work at it."

"Yeah, you work on it, cause, I sure in hell ain't goin' any damned where as tight as I am tied."

"We have no horses now, not going anywhere too fast anyway. Maybe, wild animals *will*, eat us."

"We'll have one horse shortly."

Bone looked at him like he was delirious, "What?"

"Nick'll be round shortly."

"You think he will come back?"

"I know he will."

Bone wiggled and twisted, but was having little success. After a while, sure enough Nick show up, he came trotting back and Bone's horse was following close behind. Apparently, the cactus had worked its way out. Abe whistled and called, "Come here, Nick." The horse walked slowly to where Abe was sitting on the ground, immediately Nick started sniffing curiously at the straps that Abe was wrapped tightly in. Nick started nibbling and tugging on them. "That's it Nick, pull'm off. Yeah, that's it." The horse got a piece of the strap loose and started chewing on it.

After a while the horse chewed the loose strap in two, then he chewed and pulled on another and after the second strap was in two pieces, he stepped back as if to say, 'there you go, the rest is up to you'. Abe tried to encouraged Nick to do more. The horse came back and sniffed the bindings again, then backed up shaking his head and snorting.

"Bone," Abe said, "lean against me, and I will lean against you, then we'll try to standup together."

The men tried it several times, but failed. Finally, they both were on their feet, though a bit unbalanced. Bone's hands were behind his back, so Abe told him to turn and try to unwrap him. Bone did, and at first, the straps just overlapped each other in a tangle, after working at it for quite some time they started to unwind. Abe, started shifting around and gradually the straps loosened enough, so that he could unwrap himself with his hands. It felt truly good to be free, because he had been wrapped so tight. When he was completely loose he quickly started untying Bone.

"I can't believe Balestine left our guns here," said Abe.

"He is a strange man. Got a colder heart than me."

"You're not as heartless as you think, Bone." Bone ignored Abe's comment.

After the two gathered their guns, checked and cleaned the dirt out of them, Abe said, "We'll bury the boy and then see if we can catch up with Balestine again."

"We will be more cautious this time. He is far ahead," said Bone. "I feel bad that I let a white man like Balestine get the drop on us so easy. I liked Zan; he died brave."

"Yes, yes he did. I'm gonna see that man in his grave."

Though the ground was relatively soft, it was hard digging with tree limbs. Once they had a hole, a little over two foot deep, they move Zan over and laid him to rest in it. They pushed and scooped with their hands all the dirt they could over him and then finished covering the grave with stones.

Abe stood up, and as he brushed himself off as best he could and removed his hat he said, "Sure am tarred of buryin' folks." Bone remove his hat too, following Abe's actions curiously. Abe started, "We-l-l, don't have much to say about this young man. Like Bone said, he did die bravely. Well Lord, I reckon Zan...Zander is in your hands now." Abe frowned, jerked his head a couple of nods, and put his hat back on his head. Abe tightened his jaw, "Let's get after that low-down, butcherin' vermin." Bone nodded and they went to the horses and mounted up.

They continued following the wagon tracks, which seldom left the road. From the cuts, that the wheels were making in the road, the wagon was moving at a faster, steadier pace. Each time they came to a bend in the road or a place where a person could duck out of sight, they approached with extreme caution. They followed into the night, until they could hardly see the road at all. It was an exceptionally dark night, with no moon shinning, so, it was not safe to go any farther. They camped, ate light, mostly because, most of their food stuffs was on Zaner's horse. Thay rested in shifts until break of dawn.

After coffee, warmed in a skillet, they were back on the road, chewing on a couple hardtack biscuits. May had made them with bacon grease, so they did have a little flavor. Two hours down the road, it took a wide swing right, around a grove of tall trees and underbrush. When they got around the long bend in the road, Bone stopped. He dismounted his horse, walked ten to fifteen feet off the road and checked the trail behind a large cluster of high scrub-brush. "Looks like he stopped here for a while and rested. Not for long though, I would say, 30, 40 minutes at most. It is going to take some time to catch up again."

Bone mounted up and they continued. There was only one more spot they found where Balestine had stopped and rested for a short period.

It was dark, when Abe and Bone rode into the little trading post, way-station area of Cougar Creek Ford, sixty-five miles south west of Denver.

"Abe," said Bone, as he pointed toward a little blacksmith shop that was lit up by a forge fire and a half-dozen lanterns. Abe looked and saw what Bone was bringing to his attention; it was Balestine's wagon sitting at the side of the building, with a crudely made wooden for sale sign on the seat.

They reined their horses over to the little barn. Slowly, watchfully the two dismounted, one at a time. The barns double doors were wide open. There was a large burly man with sandy red hair and mustache, wearing a thick hide apron over his clothes. He was working on a cherry red wagon part he had just pulled out of a coke forge fire with a set of tongs. He took, the almost white-hot piece, holding it firmly with the tongs, and positioned it on the anvil he was working at, and started shaping it with a large heavy hammer. Though, he was aware the two men were standing there, he paid them little mind as he noisily hammered the iron into what he wanted as sparks shot about. After a bit, he quenched it in a tub of water close by. As he held the wagon part up and admired it he said, "My name's Mike Dandre. Make you boys a real good deal on that wagon ya was lookin' at…as soon as I get this here tongue cap back on." Mike shoved the wagon part back into the hot coals and pumped the bellows a half-dozen times with his muscular left arm, the coals flamed up bright and super-hot.

Abe's expression was serious, "When'd you get it?"

"Oh, around ten this mornin'" said Mike. "Bought it off a fella that didn't want to wait, while I made a new tongue cap for it."

"That a fact? Was this man short, well built,

with a slicked downed and well-groomed beard?"

The big man's jaw became rigid, his dark eyes and wrinkled brow, displayed an air of suspicion. There was little doubt that you didn't want to be on this big man's bad side. "What's it matter to you, what this fella looked like? I generally don't discuss who my customers are, unless, I got a real good reason."

"Mike, my name is Abe Wallace. I am a US Federal Marshal, Bone here is my deputy." Abe opened his vest revealing his badge. "The man who sold you that wagon, has murdered at least three people that I know of. Two women and a young man we had to bury on the road. We don't care nothin' about that wagon, but I do aim to see him hang for what he has done. Mike, you seem like an honest man, anything you can tell me about him, might help us bring him to justice, and would be much appreciated."

Mike expression lightened up again, "If that's the case, then yeah. He's the one that sold me the wagon. Now, I know why he was in such an all fired hurry to sell it cheap, and get on out'a here."

"What about the horses?" asked Bone.

"Fine team, they were. I have no place to keep horses very long, so I sent him over to Happy Jack's Trading Post." Mike nodded toward the trading post building. "I figgered somebody over there would be interested in buyin'm. Happy, runs the relay for the stage and serves liquor over there. Farmers and cowhands like to hang around and talk. Not a man that should drink myself, I get rowdy when I drink. My misses don't like it none. I'd bet, he found a buyer over there. Might be, Happy bought'm himself. He's got a nice barn and cabin behind the trading post."

"Well, thank ya Mike. Any chance he's still around?"

"I really wouldn't know. I paid no mind after he left here. Been busy, shoed three horses today. Now, I'm tryin' to get this part done, so's I kin get home to the misses."

Is there a place we can get a decent meal and hole-up for the night?"

"Happy Jack's got that small cabin attached to the barn, he lets it out to people som'time. Don't think it's occupied right now."

"Appreciate your help, Mike. Thank you. We-l-l Bone, let's go get us a drink and see if we can find out what happened to that murderin' butcher." Bone nodded to Abe and then to Mike.

Abe started to click Nick forward, but then reined back. "Mike, there any chance you got a way to feed and put up our horses for a while, maybe for the night, if need be?"

"Yeah, there's a small corral behind the barn here; hay and feed's back there too. You can put'm there if you'll strip'm down and feed them yourselves. I will let ya keep'm there for four bits a piece; I gotta get this work done before the misses comes down here and drags me home."

After they got the horses taken care of, Abe and Bone walked down to Happy Jack's Trading Post. The evening air was cooling fast and Abe rubbed his arms with his hands vigorously. "Might just have to buy us some coats, Bone."

"Good whisky will warm us."

Abe pushed open the heavy wooden door, him and Bone stepped into the place. In short order, they realized why the owner, who was standing behind a make-shift bar (a rough-cut, four foot by eight-foot wooden slab across two large barrels) was tagged, Happy Jack. "Well, howdy my friends. Happy Jack's the name and sellin' an' tradin's the game. Come on in an' look around. If I ain't got it, I'll kill it fer ya, hee-hee...fer new customers, the first drinks on the house. Damned good, untainted, Canadian whisky. After that, you'll have to pay a premium price, cause I shore the hell know you'll want another shot or two."

Bone, gave a slight smile, or as much of a smile as Bone could give as he looked around and inspected the room full of merchandise, "Yes, Canadian whisky. Good."

Abe nodded as he looked around the place and stepped up to the slab. "Mighty fine of ya to give the Canadian. Two, one for my friend here and one for me. How much for the second, and maybe, a third?"

"For you fellas, it'll be four bits a shot. Now, that's a big shot, since I don't have no littlun's, hee-hee."

Abe, smiled and took a half step back while Happy Jack poured two small tin cups three quarters full from a dark brown unlabeled bottle. "I'd hope so— how much would it be for any other fellas?"

"Why...ah...four bits a shot. Hee-hee."

"Thought so," Abe tossed a silver dollar on the slab. Happy Jack picked up the dollar and put it between his teeth to see if it was really silver, then he dropped it into a small tin box behind him on a shelf.

"I thank ya pard, what else kin I do to lighten your load of heavy silver, hee-hee?"

Bone, came up to the slabbed bar, picked up the tin cup and threw down its contents in one swallow. "Again."

"Shore, good whisky, ain't it?" Happy Jack said as he poured another for him.

Bone nodded and threw down the second, "Again."

"Thirsty fella, huh? Hee-hee."

Abe sipped his down quickly and sat the cup down on the slab and nodded to Happy Jack, who still had the bottle in his hand. "Shore," he said and poured Abe a second cup.

"I'm lookin' to buy us a couple of winter coats. And, I'd like to get a little information from ya."

Happy Jack's smile disappeared into a more serious straight lipped stare as he leaned forward. "We-l-l, talk's cheap. But, sometimes information can cost a bit."

Abe pulled back his vest to reveal the US Federal Marshal's badge pinned on his shirt. "A fella came in here earlier today to sell a couple horses. A short, stout man, with a slicked beard, well kept. You remember him?"

"Well friend, that badge don't count for

much around here, prob'ly not another badge within, fifty…sixty mile or better. So, we pretty well mete out our own justice." Happy Jack pulled a Walker Colt out of his belt and laid it on the slab. "If you know what I mean. Yeah, it's old, and so am I, but it'll make a mighty big hole in a fella." Happy Jack noticed something from the corner of his eye, to his right, it was Bone's Remington, he cocked it.

"Oh…No, I wasn't figgerin' on usin' it with you fellas. I just wanted to let you know, how most around here handle their differences."

"Just wanted to let you know," said Bone, "I have a big hole maker also."

Happy Jack moved his hand away from the big Colt. "Yeah, shore. I bought those horses myself, good investment. I figgered, don't see nice stock like that around here too often. I added them to the team of four I got back in the barn, I find two more and I'll have two team of relief horses fer the stage. Ther stolen, huh?" Happy Jack, tilted his head back away from the barrel of Bone's Remington. It was very hard to talk with it pointed at his head ready to fire. "Hey, would you tell yer friend, Cochise here, to put that pistol away. I don't have no ill will t'ward you fellas."

"Oh…Bone. It's okay. Put it away."

Bone planted the pistol back in place. "Whisky," he said.

"Shore…hee-hee. On the house, friend." Happy Jack poured out of the bottle again, nearly filling both cups.

Abe took a sip, Bone downed his in one gulp, then another and banged the tin on the slab, "Again."

"Shore." Happy Jack poured three quarters in Bones tin cup once again.

"Good." Bone took the tin and left the bar to look around.

"No," Abe continued, "The horses are yers, fair enough. What, I need to know is, where he was headed after he left here?"

"That's an easy'n, hee-hee. I won't even charge ya for that one. Sold him two tickets…a ticket for the stage to Denver, and a train ticket to Wyomin', Credence"

"A ticket to Denver? Where do you catch the stage?"

"Right here. Left around noon. Won't be around again fer two weeks."

"So, there is a train from Denver to Wyoming?"

"Yup, goes right in to Credence. Do you mind, can I have my Colt back?"

"Yeah, sure."

"Thanks." Happy Jack took the Walker and pushed the pistol back into his belt. "Oh…four bits fer yer friend's whisky?"

"Alright," Abe replied and downed what was left in his own cup and set it back on the bar. "I believe I'll have me another." He pulled out one more silver dollar and laid it on the slab.

Happy Jack took it and tossed it into the tin box and poured Abe's tin cup almost full, the bottle was empty now. "No worry," smiled Happy Jack, "Ther's more where that came from."

Abe took a long sip from the tin cup and then downed the rest. "I'm gonna look around, need to find a good coat."

"If yer lookin' for a really good coat, look at the one hangin' on the wall there." Happy Jack pointed. "Heavy corduroy, and a buf'lo hide collar…brand spankin' new. Kin make a real deal on that one. A trapper ordered it, and got eet by a bear before he got back for it. Looks yer size."

Abe went over and tried it on, it fit perfect. "How much ya need?"

"Twelve dollars."

"Twelve dollars, are ya kiddin'?"

"It's, brand new, fifteen dollars from

Denver, buf'lo collar."

"Alright, I'll give ya six."

"SIX? Hell, no. Ten?"

"Eight's, all I'll do."

"You do fill it out better'n anyone around here. I don't know if I'll find anybody else that fits it. So-o, I-ight, it's yers for eight."

Abe brought the coat over and laid it across the slabbed bar. "Whatever, Bone brings up, I'll cover."

"Shore thing," replied Happy Jack.

Bone, had put on a colorfully patterned and beaded, horse hair, Indian vest and brought a fringed buckskin jacket over to the bar. He started to pull a poke out of his belt when, Abe stopped him and said, "No Bone, I got this." Bone nodded.

"Well, Jack what's the damage?"

"Okay, twenty-two dollars, and I'll throw in another shot a piece."

"Sounds fair," said Abe. "I need to go back down to the blacksmith's and get the money out'a my saddle bags for ya though."

"Ain't no problem, I'll bundle these up for ya whilst yer gone." Abe turned to leave and Happy Jack poured the two tin cups up again and went to work wrapping up the two coats.

Abe had just enough time to get back to the

horses and his saddle, when two big men pushed open the big heavy door at the Trading Post and stomped into Happy Jack's.

One was a huge mountain man with long curly, peppered hair flowing out from under a well-worn, wide billed pancake hat. He was clad in skins and a long buffalo skin coat. The other man was an Indian wearing a buckskin shirt and pants, under a bear skin coat. They went straight to the bar; the big white man leaned his long rifle against the bar beside himself. The Indian, planted himself, uncomfortably close to Bone. Happy Jack, sat up two tin cups for these two new patrons and poured something from a large stoneware jug. The mountain man paid for the two of them and Happy Jack tossed the coins into the tin box.

"Haven't seen you boys for a while. Hope there's no trouble here, not like the last time, hee-hee. Don't need no ruckus," advised Happy Jack.

"Humph," snorted the Indian as he threw down the contents of the tin cup. He glared over at Bone as he wiped dribbles from his chin with his coat sleeve. Bone was hunched over the tin cup with both hands wrapped around it. He looked straight ahead and paid no mind to the big Indian next to him.

"Here now," said Happy Jack as he poured from the jug again. "This one's on me," he said, hoping to still the tension that was building in the big Indian toward Bone.

"Thanks," said the mountain man, happily.

Without turning away from his glare at Bone, the Indian, took his tin and threw it down. He banged the tin hard on the wood slab. Bone didn't even flinch, though it was quite obvious that the big man was trying to get a rise out of him.

"Humph," snorted the Indian again. "Pour, Jack," he growled without taking his eyes off of Bone.

"Look you fellas, I don't want no ruckus in here tonight, understand?"

The big white man nodded and threw down his drink, making a sourer face afterward. The Indian's eyes narrowed and burned cold and dark at Bone. The big Indian struck his chest with a fist, "I am Otaktay— Lakota, great nephew of Sitting Bull, son of Chatan. You...you are stinking dog, Apache? You have, no right to wear that vest, yellow dog, Apache pig."

Bone had just about all he could stomach of this blowhard. He downed his tin and sat it gently on the wood slab. Regrettably, because of his right-hand blind-side, he had not notice that Otaktay, had pulled a long hunting knife from his belt and held it down to his side.

"I am Blood Bone. Son-of-a-bitch...Apache. And, I have had enough of you." Bone turned jerking out his Remington. Before he could level the pistol, Otaktay, plunged the long blade into Bone's side, hitting a rib, so that knifes point glanced, and came out on the side of his back.

The thrust of the knife, caused Bone to fall down on one knee, the long knife slid back out of his side. He just melted on down to the floor with his pistol in hand. The big Indian leaned over to finish him off with the bloody knife. He was very close when, Bone's Remington spoke loud and sent the big Indian to his end, with a large, burning, gaping hole in the center of his chest, igniting the bear skin coat ablaze briefly. He fell to the side of Bone, who was still on the floor, wounded and bleeding.

The mountain man had been silent up till now, he calmly reached over, grabbed his rifle, chambered a round with a sharp metallic sound and aimed at Bone on the floor. He started squeezing the trigger. Bone raised the Remington again, and as he fired, another explosion at the same time from Happy Jack's Walker Colt, blew the mountain man's brains out the side of his head. Bones slug had hit the man in the stomach. The man smashed into the floor lifeless. When he hit the floor, the rifle went off, and sent a slug into the meaty part of Bone's lower leg.

Suddenly, the door slammed open, Abe stood there in the doorway, with a pistol's in each hand. "What the hell?"

Happy Jack hurried over to examined Bone's wounds, after a quick assessment, he said, "I think he just might live, if you'll help me get him out back to the cabin."

With the two on the floor dead, Abe put his pistols away and went to help. "Just what the hell happened here? Looks like Custer's last stand in here."

"I knew that big Indian was gonna push the wrong person one day. Hee...Hee, he did today. He goaded and pushed yer friend until he had no choice, but to respond and he did. Don't think yer friend knew he had his huntin' knife out. He's lucky it slipped off to the side, I think it hit a rib, otherwise he'd be a lot worse, mebee dead. Gonna be pretty darn sore though, especially, after I sew him up. Hated havin' ta kill ol' Kepler there, done a lot of business with'm. But, he was fixin' ta use that 45.70 to finish off yer friend.

"I need ya ta hep me geet him out back to the cabin. I kin work on'em ther."

"Sure, sure," said Abe. "Take it easy ol' friend, we'll get you fixed up."

The cabin was of a good size, with two rooms and a door to separate them. Happy Jack, told Abe to push two tables that were in the room together while he held on to Bone. "Good, now hep me geet him up on those tables and strip him down, I got some sewin' ta do."

Bone had four gaping holes in him, two in his side, where the knife had entered, glanced off a rib and the point of the long knife had come out. Then, two where the .45-70 slug entered and ripped through the calf muscle of his right leg, before tearing a large hole in the wooden plank floor.

"Ah heck, I forgot the whisky" said Happy Jack. "Kin you go back and geet the crocked jug on the bottom shelf behind the bar?"

"Certainly," Abe stood up and went to the Trading Post. Quickly finding a full jug, he returned and handed it to Happy Jack, who had Bone stripped down bare.

Abe handed him the jug and he uncorked it and took a big swig. "Now go in the other room and geet me a blanket off the bed." Abe complied.

Happy Jack told Bone to 'take a long pull from the jug' and he did; it went down harshly, nowhere near the smoothness of the Canadian.

"That is kerosene," Bone complained.

"Nope, not quite," replied Happy Jack. Then he rolled up a rag he found and said, "Bite down on this. Cause this is gonna sting a bit." Jack stuck the rag between Bone's teeth and proceeded to pour a healthy amount of the jugs contents on each of the wounds. Bone jerked and winced, but never made a sound.

Abe had returned with the blanket and covered Bone as best he could with it. "Now," said Happy Jack, "over ther, in that cabinet on the wall, you'll find some catgut and a needle. Kin ya geet it fer me?"

"Sure," Abe got it, and handed it to Jack.

Happy Jack, looked into Bone's eyes kind-heartedly, "Well friend, ya might wanna 'nother pull out'a the jug before I start sewin'. Cause this ain't gonna be no Sunday picnic fer ya."

Bone nodded, and Jack removed the rag from his mouth and offered the jug. Even though, it was probably the wickedest whisky he had ever tasted, he raised his head as Jack helped him with it. Bone, never turned down whisky, anytime, anywhere; he downed a good long swallow. When he was done, Jack laid his head back down and sat the jug on the corner of the table. He then wiped Bone's mouth with the rag and tried to put it back in his mouth, but he refused. "Okay," said Jack, "it's yer party."

Jack threaded the needle with a long piece of catgut. Then, he looked at Abe, gave a grimaced smile, nodded and went to work sewing. Bone, ground his teeth, flinched a number of times, but never uttered a sound during the whole process. Jack, offered the jug half way through, and Bone swallowed a drink and Jack continued as Abe watched.

Jack, worked quickly and it was obvious it wasn't his first doctoring. When he was done he gave Bone, who was worn out, another big swallow out of the jug. Jack, then poured what was left on the four wounds. Then he put some kind of thick salve, he got out of the cabinet on each wound. Jack wrapped Bone's leg with some white cloth that he tore in strips.

"Alright now, hep me geet him into the bed in the other room." After covering Bone in a layer of blankets, and making him as comfortable as they could, Jack said to Abe, "He's gonna need a week, mebee two, to rest and heal. And, I'll need to keep a close eye on those wounds fer infection; don't want nothin' to mess up the fine sewin' I did." Bone was sound asleep and resting. "Let's go get us some Canadian, friend," Jack said.

"Yeah, Ca-na-di-an. Got to wash that rot-gut out of my mouth," Bone mumbled with his eyes half open, and then fell back to sleep. Abe nodded, and they left Bone to rest in the cabin.

Orin Vaughn

11

Abe and Jack were back in the Trading Post and Jack went and got a new bottle of Canadian. Abe, stepped over the dead Indian and picked up the cup that was sitting on the slab when he left to go get the money out of the saddlebags, he swallowed it down. Jack came out with a new bottle of Canadian, got a tin for himself, pulled the stopper and poured a full cup for himself, then filled Abe's cup.

The two sipped on the whisky and talked. "When's that train leave Denver for Wyoming?" asked Abe.

"Tomarra mawnin', at eight o'clock."

"I'd have to ride my horse to death to make it, I suppose?"

"Purdy much so. Then I wouldn't bet on ya make'n it on time."

"How long do you think it will be before Bone's able to ride?"

"No sooner than a week as long as ther's no infection."

"When's the next train leave Denver for Wyoming?"

Happy Jack turned and pulled a train schedule from the shelf behind him and looked it over. "Ther's a freight leavin' Monday at noon."

"A freight train, huh? Monday, will give me plenty of time to get to there, no problem. You reckon I could book freight for my horse?"

"Shore it's a freight train. Thet is, if he don't mind keepin' company with a few horny prize bulls and such. Not in same car a'course."

"Well, we better settle up here. How much more do ya need for your doctorin' and takin' care of Bone till he's ready to ride? Oh, and I'll need a place to stay the night?"

"If'n ya help me stick those two hombres in a couple pine coffins I got in the barn, I'll settle fer, ah- fifty dollars in all. Don't have to bury'm, I got a kid that comes around ever' couple days and works for me."

"Fifty gonna be enough for the coats an' all."

"Shore, weren't yer friends fault that big Indian pushed him into a fight. It's my place and I do feel some responsible."

"Can I cash a bank draft in Denver? That's gonna do it for my cash. I'll have to pay for the train fair when I get the draft cashed."

"Yeah, shore. An', better bring yer horses down here. Mike don't like ta keep horses down at the blacksmith shop."

Abe decided a week or more was too long to wait in getting after Balestine, and getting up to his assignment in Wyoming was a priority. So, the three of them talked it over and they all decided it would be better, if Bone went back to Arizona. It just wasn't a good idea taking a chance on meeting up with anymore unfriendly northern tribe Indians. Bone, warned Abe to be extra careful dealing with Balestine, because he wouldn't be there to watch his back. He reminded Abe, that he was a complicated, callous soul.

As Abe rode away from the trading post to cross the ford, a young boy of about sixteen was digging the first hole for the two wooden boxes that were sitting close by where he was working. Abe gave him a nod as Nick splashed into the cold mountain water. It was a beautiful sunshiny day, but the air had a chill.

Happy Jack had given Abe a possibles bag with some jerky and hard-tack. He also threw in a bottle of Canadian and told Abe he could pay for it next time he passed through.

In Denver, Abe quickly found a bank and got the draft cashed. Then he paid for his ticket and the freight charge for Nick to Credence.

He gave the ticket clerk a description of Balestine and asked if he remembered seeing him around for the last train that had left for Wyoming. He was told that since he already had a ticket, he wouldn't have noticed him. The clerk told Abe that the conductor would have seen him, but since he was taking a freight to Wyoming, not a passenger train, it would not be the same conductor. So, Abe had no real way of knowing if Balestine was in Wyoming, however, he had his assignment and for now, that needed to be his first concern. He wasn't going to forget Balestine, he wouldn't be at ease until he was brought to justice or dead.

Abe sent a telegraph message to the Credence, Sheriff's Office to let them know when he would be arriving. The answer came back, that the Sheriff was out of town, but a deputy by the name of AJ Cutter would be there to meet him.

Though the train ride went through some amazing country, Abe caught up on some much-needed sleep on the way.

As Abe stepped down from the train and looked around, a thin middle-aged man with a peppered, bushy mustache, that seemed to cover his whole face, came up to him and asked, "Are you Federal Marshal Wallace?"

"Yeah, that's me. You can call me Abe, most do. You must be Deputy Cutter?"

"Yes sir, AJ, is what most call me," he offered a handshake. "Ya got a horse to unload, if I understood your message?"

After the two shook hands they went to the freight car where Nick was, and unloaded him. "Ya know Abe," said AJ, "we could have supplied ya a horse."

"No, not like this one. I know he might not look special, but he is. Nick's, like no other horse, I ever owned. He knows me and I know him, he's never failed to be there when I needed him."

"Well, if you say so, Abe."

"Yeah, I say so."

"Let's get, Nick, settled down at the livery, then I'll buy ya a drink over at the saloon before introducing you to the other deputy, Lanny Pane. I'll fill ya in on what's goin' on around here."

"Sounds good to me," smiled Abe. "Pleasure before pursuance." AJ laughed.

After Nick was secured, Abe and AJ were talking at a table in the Lucky Loser, a local saloon, while sharing a bucket of beer. "Here's the situation up here," started AJ, "The Sheriff doesn't spend much time here around Credence. He's usually taking care business elsewhere, lot of country to cover. And, he's into politics pretty deep, tryin' to influence the money, sort'a speak. So, keeping the peace and maintaining order around here locally, pretty well falls on me and Lanny's shoulders. And, we do alright for the most part. But, the reason I asked for outside help is, about a year ago, a few big cattlemen up here, and a large group of sheepherders, got together and formed, what they call the Stockmen's Protection League."

Abe eyebrows raised. AJ continued, "I know what you are thinking, sheep men and cattlemen don't usually mix. But, this time, because they both want to keep open range, and don't want wire, settlement farmers and small ranchers taking over free land, they're making a stand together to keep them out. At first, they just bought out those little outfits that weren't doing so good. About five months ago, they hired some gunmen, mostly from Texas. They started strong-arming small farmers and ranchers to leave. One of their top hired gun-hands by the name of John A. E. Alexander is runnin' the outfit under the pretense of bein' Masters McFerrin's ranch foreman."

"John Alexander? Yeah, yeah…, Jax," said Abe.

"Jax?"

"Yeah, that's what he goes by in Texas. He's a hired gunman that specializes in working for big outfits intimidating small ranchers. Makes his living working for the highest paying side of range disputes."

"Well, Sheriff Haskell and Masters McFerrin are good friends, politicly speakin', that is. He tells me to just do what I can, and leave Masters to him. McFerrin, owns the biggest spread around, he carries a lot of influence in the territory. I figger he's the one that brought in the Texas guns. Nothing big has happened yet, but I think it's about to. Word has it, McFerrin and the Stockmen's League has hired some special regulator, to come up here and be a persuasive motivation in getting these smaller operators to move out.

"The biggest hold out they're dealin' with is, Tom Burlington; he holds the little outfits together against the Stockmen's Protection League. When, I sent for help, I had just been forced to arrest Tom and another small rancher for rustling cattle from McFerrin's herd. I had to hold them in jail for three weeks before the circuit Judge came around. There wasn't enough evidence against them, because the charges were trumped up. They both had solid alibis, so the Judge dismissed the charges. They were mending fences all day with other small ranchers, when the cattle were supposed to have been rustled. I'm seein' this thing getting way out of hand, in short order, with these hired guns gatherin' up here. Me and Lanny's gonna have more than we can handle, I'm sure."

AJ poured the last of the beer into their glasses. The two swallowed them down and left for the Jail.

12

The Jail was a log building with a small office and two separate, very secure, riveted, strap-iron holding cells; it wouldn't be an easy place to escape from. Lanny, the other Deputy, was just coming in to work as Abe and AJ arrived. They all went inside and after introductions, Lanny routinely built a fire in the small flat-top stove and put together an all-day pot of coffee.

In a short time, they all sat around the large oak desk in the office, talking and enjoying Lanny's coffee. As they talked, Abe began forming an estimation of the two lawmen he would be working with. He sensed that Lanny was mature and resolute beyond his twenty-two years. He had been dealing with rowdy ranch hands and tough cowboys for a couple of years, and didn't seem like a man who would shrink back when in a desperate situation. AJ, was a seasoned lawman, over worked and under paid, yet a man who would stand for what was right, to the death if necessary; the kind of man you would want by your side in a standoff.

Lanny, originally from Tucson, Arizona Territory, abruptly interrupted a lull in the conversation. "Yeah...now, I remember. Yer the lawman who brought in the Zimmerman Brother's. They robbed the Tucson stage and killed one of the passengers. I was young then, but I remember you riding down the street behind them two, you had a shotgun across your lap. Them boys were hung a few weeks later. I knew you looked familiar."

"I'm sure the hell a bit older now," said Abe.

"Yeah, but yer still a lawman to be reckoned with, a man of reputation," replied Lanny.

"Well, thanks for your confidence. I hope I live up to your expectations."

"I have no doubt ya can."

"How about we address the issues before us here," said AJ. "There'll be plenty of time for commendation, after we get this potential range war under control."

"Yeah," said Abe. "You know, I've got a strong hunch about who your hired, special regulator, might be."

"Yeah well, how would you have any insight on that?" asked AJ.

Abe, explained what Balestine looked like, and told the story of his dealings with him since leaving May's place.

AJ shook his head, "This fella's a threat to our good citizens. We need to find him before he starts a holy terror around here."

Lanny recalled, "That sounds like the man that Milo the bartender, down at the Lucky Loser Saloon, described to me yesterday. The man was looking to buy a wagon and a couple of good horses, he told me."

"Where do you suppose, he sent him?" questioned Abe, "Cause that's, sure enough Balestine. He don't ride horses, he likes to travel around in a wagon with a good set of horses."

"He sent him down to the Credence Livery."

"From what you told us," contended AJ, "we'd better catch up with him as soon as possible. Don't want him to start killin' folks around here."

The three left the Jail and headed for the livery, talking and getting better acquainted as they walked. When they met with the livery owner, he acknowledged that indeed, a man answering to Balestine's description had bought a medium sized, high sided wagon and two horses from him, late the previous evening. The man at the livery, also told them that Balestine, didn't care for the quality of the horses he sold him. He had asked where he could purchase a better pair, and was told that the Burlington Ranch had good stock and could probably find something there more to his liking. The Burlington place was about eight miles out of town.

On their way back down the street, they saw someone running toward them who appeared to be in quite a frenzy. It turned out to be Milo the saloon keeper. "AJ…AJ," he was calling. The three stopped and waited.

Milo, a tall, slim, well dress fellow in a fancy stitched buttoned up vest and string tie came up and literally fell into AJ's arms.

"What in hell's got you so fired up and out of breath, Milo?"

"It…it's, Jenny Childers," gasp Milo.

"Yeah, what about Jenny?"

"I—I found her dead. Dead, up in her room. Wh-e-e-w, AJ. Danged horrible. Throat cut…, and her beautiful red hair, all chopped off. Never seen nothin' like it before."

"What? What the hell?" said AJ. AJ and Lanny gave Abe a distasteful look and AJ accused, "You— You, chased that muderin' son-of-a-bitch up here." Milo and Lanny both had a sweet spot for Jenny, but the feelings weren't mutual for either.

"What are you talkin' about?" defended Abe. "I never chased him nowhere. He was on his way up here when I came along. You want to blame someone for him being here, you'd better start with this so-called Stockmen's Protection League."

"Yeah. Well, sorry," apologized AJ. "Let's go down and see what we can find out about this. I want this Balestine fella's boots swinging in the wind, with his neck stritchin' at the end of a rope."

The three-some headed for Lucky Loser to investigate the murder. When they got there, Abe went around back to the alley to see if he could find any clues of how Balestine might have snuck in unobserved. AJ and Lanny went to the upstairs room to view the pitiful sight of the young dance hall girl named, Jenny Childers.

As Abe suspected, he found wagon tracks and signs that the horse team had stood in place for a while. There was an outside stairway that went up to a landing that ran the length of the building and gave access to the rooms up there. It was obvious that this was the way Balestine had stolen in and carried out his despicable deed. What AJ and Lanny found, was pretty much what Milo had described to them; a gruesome sight. Her hands had been bound with leather straps, other than that, there were no sign of much of a struggle. AJ, made arrangements for Jenny's body to be discreetly removed and taken to the undertaker.

Back at the Jail, AJ slammed himself into the chair behind the desk; he leaned forward and forcefully pounded the desk top with both his fist and roared, "I want this son-of-a-bitch caught and killed or hung. There's no need for such an animal to continue livin'."

"I agree," said Abe. "We need to go out and talk to this Burlington fella and see if he knows anything about where Balestine might be hole up after buying those horses."

AJ looked at Lanny, "Yeah, you two go ahead out there and see what you can find out. I'll go back down to the Lucky Loser and ask around, to see if anyone knows anything about this madman."

Abe and Lanny were on their way out of town when they met Masters McFerrin, the man named Jax and three other ranchers belonging to the Stockmen's Protection League.

They all stopped facing one another before they passed. McFerrin's outfit took up the whole narrow road leading into town, and, it didn't seem they were going to give up much of it to let Abe and Lanny pass.

"Good mornin'," said McFerrin. Lanny nodded. "What are you up to today, Deputy?"

"Official business," replied Lanny coolly.

"Yeah, we're investigating a murder, Mr. McFerrin," said Abe. "The killer's someone I think you're already acquainted with, Salmon Balestine."

"Nope, don't know anyone by that name. Why would I be acquainted with any murderer? Who are you anyway, mister?"

"Me? I'm Abe Wallace, US Federal Marshal," Abe gestured to the badge on his vest. "Funny you don't know him, he's supposed to be up here to work as a special regulator to help motivate the small ranchers around here to move on."

"Never heard the name before," said McFerrin casually.

"How 'bout you Jax? Someone, maybe you recruited?" The three ranchers looked at McFerrin and Jax curiously.

"Not me, Wallace. Al'm justa workin' man."

"Yeah," said McFerrin, "He's my new foreman."

"Sure, he is. I know what his business is. Jax, I don't think you wanna get tangled up in this one. Not with this woman killer, Balestine, as a working partner."

"That a fact?" replied Jax calmly. He leaned forward in the saddle. "Don't know nothin' about no, Balestan."

"Balestine, Jax. Oh, I think y'all know more than you're sayin'. I believe, if I were you fellas, I'd lighten up, at least until we bring this varmint to justice. Mr. McFerrin, your so called, Stockman's Protection League, ought to be more careful about who they hire as a regulator."

"Regulator? I told you, I don't know who you're talkin' about. Nobody, by that name, is under my employment," McFerrin insisted.

"I would hope not," said Abe, "Cause that would make you an accessory to murder."

McFerrin wrinkled his face, "Who the hell got murdered anyway?"

Fiery, Lanny struck out like a rattler, "Sweet little Jenny Childers, that's who."

McFerrin's face went void, then his eyes narrowed. "Damn… I'm sorry to hear that," he said bleakly.

"So," asked Abe, "Do you know the where-a-bouts of Balestine?"

Stiffly McFerrin said, "I told you, I don't know anything about this individual." He spurred his horse forward. "Let's go men," ordered McFerrin, and the group pushed their way past the two lawmen on the narrow road, giving them a hard look as each man rode by.

13

Abe and Lanny, continued on the road toward the Burlington Ranch. The road was narrow, lined with blue spruce and others trees that were just starting to change into their impressive fall colors. Finally, the road widened and a mile or so later they turned off onto a long lane that lead to some fenced land and a double open gate with a large log overhead frame. The lane leads up to a ranch house and barn.

As they passed through the gate, Nick baulked and pawed the ground as he snorted. "Somethings not right up there," said Abe as he nodded toward the house.

"Yeah, it seems unusually quiet," agreed Lanny.

They approached slowly, cautiously, observing every movement. There were a number of horses, all different sizes, in a fenced field to their left, and a small herd of sheep to the right. Nick was prancing anxiously as they continued forward; Abe had no doubt something was seriously wrong up ahead. When the two men came around the corner, to the north side of the barn, their suspicions slammed them full force in the face to a terrible reality.

Sixteen-year-old Tanner Burlington, was sitting on a log from a nearby wood pile. His mother's head was in his lap; she was dead, half undressed, her throat cut and most of her long black curly hair had been crudely chopped off. Leather straps were laying nearby, Tanner had probably had untied her hands. About three feet away, lay young, thirteen-year-old Gloria, her hands bound in leather straps. She was in much the same shape as her mother, with her throat cut and her hair chopped off.

Tanner looked up at the two men as they stepped down from their horses. Eyes red, silent tears streaming down his face; he looked deep into Abe's eyes and shaking his head slowly, he questioned sorrowfully, "Why? Why would...?" Tanner's emotions would not allow him to speak any further.

"I really don't know son. I really don't know," said Abe.

Abe heard an odd noise, and looked in the direction of the sound. It was Lanny, bent over and vomiting harshly at the side of the barn. When Lanny noticed Abe was looking his way, he shook his head apologetically, holding up a finger, indicating he would be done shortly.

"No need to apologize," said Abe. "I would, if I hadn't seen so much slaughter during the war."

Lanny, straightened up and went over and made a futile effort to comfort Tanner. Abe, looked about and tried to piece together what had taken place.

There were signs that a wagon had been parked in the barn lot for a length of time, there was no doubt in his mind, it had been Balestine's wagon. From other markings in the dirt in the lot, it look as though the horses on the wagon had been changed out.

Little Tommy, was lying face down in the dirt with a large caliber bullet hole in the back of his head, he hadn't known what hit him. It was obvious, he had been running toward his father when shot. Tom Burlington, apparently had been chopping wood and had started back to work, maybe, after making a deal on the horses and switching them out. Apparently, he was going for his rifle leaning against the side of the barn, when he was shot twice in the back. Both, Mrs. Burlington and her daughter, had been molested.

Lanny, took Tanner in the house to get cleaned up, Abe continued to look around for clues that would prove Balestine was the culprit in this slaughter. He wondered where Tanner had been when this had taken place; it was quite obvious he hadn't been there.

The only real evidence that it had Balestine was the wagon tracks. It was frustrating for Abe not to have some kind of hard proof that Balestine had committed this horrible act of mayhem and murder. He examined the wagon and horse tracks again, hoping to find some clue. As he searched every inch of the tracks in the dust of the lot, he wished Bone was there. Then he spotted something. Apparently, one of the rear wagon wheels had a chunk missing from the side of the metal rim and had made a rather conspicuous triangle shaped, built up in the dirt. It was of fair size, about an inch and a half, he wondered why he hadn't noticed it before. He followed the wheel track back a way and seen that, once in a while, a chunk of dirt that had been packed in the cavity would fall out making a mold of the impression. Abe found one that had been tightly packed together with dirt and manure. He gently picked it up. He went over to a water trough by the well pump and after wrapping it up in his neckerchief, he moistened it ever so lightly, to hold it together. He knew that when it dried it would be firm enough to hold together.

Now Abe was anxious to get back to town and examine the wagon tracks behind the saloon. He hoped at least some would be left, for he expected the traffic behind the saloon was pretty light.

Lanny and Tanner came out of the house, Tanner looked a little better, though he was still distraught over the death of his family. "Tanner said," explained Lanny, "there is a place where we can bury his family behind the house. It's fenced in, his Aunt is buried back there. There's a pick and shovels in the barn."

The three of them worked for about two hours getting all of them in the ground. Tanner stopped numerous times to break down not able to continue. After the graves were all covered over and four crude wooden markers were made, they solemnly stood by the graves silently.

Tanner was the one to break the silence after a long while. "I'll buy proper markers in town."

"Shouldn't someone say some words?" Lanny questioned.

Tears rolled down Tanner's face. "I wouldn't know what to say. 'cept, I hope we catch the som-bitch that done this."

"I ain't much on prayin'", said Abe. "But,

I'll say something." After he paused for a moment, struggling to find some word he said, "Hope these folks rest peaceably, until the Good Lord decides what he wants to do with them. And, I...I ask that we might find and punish the one responsible for this atrocity."

Tanner had been out tending sheep with the neighbors all night as they grazed in some high grass pasturage some miles away. He had left his horse to wonder after he dismounted in the barn lot. The horse, they found behind the house, nibbling on some tender grass.

Abe placed the dirt mold from the wagon wheel in his saddlebag carefully, so as, not to get crushed on their way back to town.

It was a slow ride back to town. Tanner spoke little, he did keep repeating the question, 'Why?'. It wasn't an easy thing to lose your whole family in one day. From what brief conversation there was between Lanny and Tanner, Abe gathered that Tanner's older brother, Tom, had been killed in a logging accident, just a little less than a year ago. Later, Abe learned from Lanny, that Tanner had been leading two draft horses up a steep hill while pulling a very large log, the chain broke and the log rolled down the hill and over Tom, killing him. Though, everyone tried to convince him otherwise, Tanner blamed himself for his brother's death.

When they got to town they found that AJ had left to investigate a shooting. Pop Lovell, a local small cattle rancher, had been shot off his horse from behind with a large caliber pistol, just outside of town about two miles. A farmer had been on his way into town for supplies, and found him on the road. He came on into town and reported what he found to AJ.

Pop, a testy old man, was a well-known advocate of small ranchers and everyone knew his firm stand against the Stockmen's Protection League. He even once beat two members severely with a heavy cane he carried. He had accused them of destroying his fences. He was arrested and paid a substantial fine for the deed. Unfortunately, there was no proof that they had been the ones who pulled down his fence.

Lanny went into the Jail and wrote a full report about the murders at the Burlington ranch, and left it where AJ could find it.

"You two wait here. I'll be back shortly," Lanny told Abe and Tanner, then he stormed out of the office.

Abe didn't think too much of it at the time. His mind was occupied with getting down behind the saloon and seeing if he could find any matching wheel tracts. He poured some coffee and offered Tanner a cup, he declined the offer. Later, Abe found out that Lanny had went over to the Stockmen's Hall and confronted McFerrin and the others about the slaughter at the Burlington ranch. McFerrin denied any knowledge of it of course. Lanny, threatened the whole group with a reckoning, if he found they had been involved in anyway.

Lanny, came in and slammed the door behind him and scowled, "'em sons-a-bitches."

"Who?" asked Abe.

"Those damned, Stockmen. That's who."

"Calm down boy, we'll get this worked out soon, I'm sure."

"It better be dog-gone soon."

"I wanna get down to the saloon and check out those wagon tracks."

"Yeah," said Lanny. "I'm ready for some drinkin'. Com'on Tanner." Tanner got up and sheepishly followed Lanny.

Abe was anxious to get down to the rear of the Lucky Loser Saloon to check for matching wagon wheel tracks. Lanny and Tanner went there also, but not to help find tracks. They went in the front door.

Orin Vaughn

14

The alley had been pretty well traveled by a lot of traffic. However, where the wagon had been setting for a while, Abe found what he needed. Sure enough, plainly, there was a clear impression of the triangle in the damage wheel that matched perfect. There was no doubt in Abe's mind now, Balestine was the one responsible for the carnage.

When Abe went into the Lucky Loser, Lanny and Tanner were into a well-oiled, mind numbing, drinking bout. The saloon was lively, jumping with piano music, dancing girls and a full breasted singing gal. She wore a bright red dress and petticoat, which she fanned at the cowboys exposing her lifted heeled shoes, pink bloomers and checkered black stockings; when she did this, the men shouted and cheered her on as she belted out songs like, 'Oh Susanna'.

Most all the patrons, were hired hands of the big ranchers, all members of the Stockmen's Protection League. Abe recognized a number of the men as hired gunmen he had met at one time or another in his travels across the country. It had cooled off a bit outside and Abe had put his coat on and it covered his badge. Nobody, paid him much attention since, there were a lot of new faces in town. He bellied up to the bar beside two cowboys that were talking. When the barkeep came up and asked, 'what he would have?', he said, "A double shot of good Canadian, if ya got it."

"Yup," said the barkeep, "be four bits."

Abe tossed a silver dollar on the bar and said, "Wait. And, you can pour me another."

"Shore."

"In fact," said Abe, "leave the bottle."

"Yup. Four dollars."

Abe pulled three more silver dollars out of his poke and dropped them into the barkeeps hand. "Yup," said the barkeep and he walked away to the cash box.

Abe sipped his whiskey as the two fellas next to him talked. There was no discretion in their tenor or how loud they talked.

"Yeah, sent his ass up north to that hunter's cabin on the Wood River. Shore wasn't no need of all that other crap; all he had to do was take care of the men. Mr. McFerrin's really ticked, 'specially about Jenny. Wouldn't surprise me if he don't send somebody up there ta kill that som'bitch."

"Me neither, that ol' fart were pretty fonda that gal."

"Hell yes, she was a purdy'un."

"That 'er lady doin' the singin' ain't half bad neither."

"Yeah, let's wonder on over an' take a closer look."

The two cowboys left the bar and joined the crowd. Abe, wonder about their conversation. Could they have been talking about Balestine he wondered? 'Surely, it was'. He knew it had to be. He decided to take his bottle and share what he had heard with AJ down at the Jail. He slapped the cork back in the bottle and left the saloon.

When Abe stepped into the office, AJ was at the desk, feet propped up, his head buried behind a newspaper. "Got a couple of glasses handy? Got some good whisky to share with you, and, some interesting information I just overheard down at the saloon about the whereabouts of ol', Salmon Balestine."

AJ jerked the newspaper down and let his chair slam to the floor. He threw some old coffee out of a tin cup on the desk toward a coal bucket and said, "Another cup's on the shelf, by the gun rack. Let's hear what you got."

Abe blew dust out of the cup and pulled up a stool to the desk opposite AJ, uncorked the bottle and poured. "I was at the bar and overheard a conversation of two cowboys that work for McFerrin."

AJ removed the tin cup down from his mouth, "Yeah, well, what'd you hear?" he impatiently asked.

"You know anything about a hunters cabin up on a— Wood River?"

"Yeah. McFerrin had it built for when he goes up north to hunt elk. Never been up there myself though. Problem with that is, if he's there, it's out of our jurisdiction. Besides, I can't leave now, not with all the trouble brewin' between these ranchers."

Abe leaned forward toward AJ, his brow creased and eyes hard, "Well, it sure the hell ain't out of my jurisdiction. All I need is a map that shows me how to get there."

"You goin' up there by yourself?"

"Don't look like I got much of a choice. I want that animal brought in, dead or alive. The wagon tracks I found out at the Burlington ranch are positive proof that Balestine is responsible for that slaughter."

"I'll have the local justice swear out a warrant right away," assured AJ.

"That would be good. I'll get ready to go and leave in the morning; I don't need no warrant for that no count animal. You go ahead and get that warrant in hand, it will be good to have it when I get back with that mangy dog."

"Aright," said AJ. "Watch yerself though. From what you told me of him, he's a slippery buzzard."

"Yeah, thanks. I won't let him get away from me again."

Abe pulled his flask from inside his vest pocket and filled it from the bottle on the desk and set it back down. "Enjoy the rest, AJ."

"Yeah, I will, thanks."

Abe went to the door and opened it. "I mean it. You be careful, Abe. That's hard territory up there, and I don't mean, just because of the rough country."

Abe looked back, "Yeah...I understand. Thanks."

When Abe got to the livery stable to get things ready for the next morning's journey, he met Lanny and Tanner mounting up. Both were snookered and sharing a bottle.

"Gonna ride with Tanner back to his home," slurred Lanny.

"Yeah...ho-m-m-me swe—et hommm," said Tanner, struggling to get on his horse.

"Alright fellas, take it easy. I'll be gone for a few days on some official business. I'll see you when I get back." Abe didn't want to mention Balestine in front of Tanner, so he waited until they got mounted up, with much difficulty, and headed out of town.

15

Abe rented a room above the Lucky Loser for the night. As soon as it opened the next morning, he bought a few things at the Credence General Mercantile Store; plenty of ammunition for the Lightening and his Colt Army, coffee, hard-tack, smoked bacon and a small bag of beans.

Abe had just secured everything in his saddlebags and was outside in front of livery stable. He was about to climb up into the saddle on Nick's back, when Lanny, came into town leading Tanner's horse with the limp body of Tanner across his back.

Abe went to the body on the horse and examined it. "What happened Lanny? How'd Tanner die?"

"I killed him, shore as hell."

"What are you talkin' about, Lanny?"

"I should have known young Tanner couldn't handle all that drinkin'. Should have had him sleep it off in the Jail. Never should have let him head for home last night." Lanny had tears rolling down his face. "Yeah, should have known better. All my fault."

Abe put his hand on Lanny's shoulder, "Just what happened boy? Tell me how Tanner died?"

"Well, we drank a lot down at the Lucky Loser. Then, Tanner wanted to go home. I tried to get him to stay in town for the night, he insisted on goin' home though. I said, I'd go with him then. He bought a bottle to take along. I shouldn't a let'm, darn-it. We rode slow, takin' our time. I took a nip or two from the bottle, Tanner, he nursed it all the way out; and when we turned down the lane to the ranch, I heard him moan. I looked back to see what was wrong."

The moon was bright as day in a clear sky, it was day-light. Lanny was weeping now. "Tanner's eyes just rolled back in his head and he fell backward off his horse, he hit the ground hard, broke his danged neck. It's my fault for takin' him to drink at the saloon. I thought it would lighten the shock of losing his whole family. It's just my durn fault."

"Maybe," said Abe. "And, maybe it would have happened anyway. Can't never tell about these things. I wouldn't be too hard on yourself; People live, and people die, just the way things flow sometimes. Nothing we can do or say changes that. I mean, I don't know that people have a time to die, I just know they do. It ain't necessarily nobody's fault, unless we kill'm outright. We just grieve a bit and go on with or own lives."

Tears that had rolled down Lanny's cheeks, gathered dust on his face and made it look like two horrible jagged scares; he snuffed up his emotions a bit, "I appreciate yer words, but I still feel responsible for him dying."

Abe helped Lanny make arrangements for Tanner to be buried out at their homestead, then he made sure Lanny was sleeping sound in the Jail after an explanation to AJ. After that was all taken care of, he checked and made sure everything was secured and mounted up and headed north.

AJ, had never been up to the cabin, only to Arland once, so the directions he gave were pretty crude. It was mostly follow the road up to Arland and after that he was pretty well on his own. After claiming he was a friend of Masters McFerrin and saying he had permission to use the cabin for hunting and fishing, he asked around in Arland and got directions. One fellow, informed him that he thought someone was already up there, using the cabin. Abe just kind of shrugged it off as of no concern.

16

Abe, was a little less than a day's travel from Credence, with Balestine in the back of a wagon, shackled down. Abe was exhausted, the weather was bone chilling, spitting icy snow all the way. He hadn't gotten much rest at night, knowing how cunning Balestine could be. He nodded off as the night, almost black, began to creep dark purple and blue through the mountains. Blowing ice crystals stung his face as the horses trudged along pulling the wagon; he didn't want to, but it was time to stop, he was cold, hungry and tired.

Balestine, laid still trying to keep warm, wrapped up in blankets, he wasn't asleep though. He contemplated the state Abe was in, knowing that his usual alertness was worn from the weather, the long trip and his lack of rest. He realized, if he was going to make a move to escape, it would have to be soon or he would have no more opportunities. So, his mind got busy scheming how to overpower Abe and free himself.

Abe pulled the wagon off the road to a little clearing, partly surrounded by some fair-sized trees. He held up under a large cottonwood to help shelter them from the weather. With difficulty and much effort, Abe finally rounded up enough moderately dry wood to get a fire going. He made coffee and sliced thick pieces of the last of the smoked bacon and cooked it on a stick. Balestine's feet were shackled tight around a large, heavy, downed cottonwood limb.

The two were sipping coffee after they had eaten when, Balestine insisted, "Abie...I need to go. Right now, Abie."

Irritated and mean eyed, Abe responded, "Awe hell, Balestine. Can't you let me finish my coffee first?"

"No. I have necessity now, Abie."

Abe took a long sip of his coffee and stepped over to unshackle one of Balestine's feet. He knelt down on one knee and unlocked one foot. The chain was still under the heavy log and Abe started to pull it out; suddenly, Balestine slung the wrist shackles over Abe's head and pulled them tight around his neck. He put his loose foot on Abe's shoulder and pushed him around so that now, he was leveraging behind his back with his knee and pulling the chain tight, choking the breath right out of Abe. Abe felt his wind pipe starting to collapse, he was panicked and knew he only had and instant to react or he would be dead. His breath was gone, when the chain lightened from around his neck, he gasped in a lung full of air as he felt Balestine's muscular left forearm slip around his neck replacing the chain. Once again, Abe's air was cut off, he felt Balestine's right hand searching his hip for his holstered Colt. Abe frantically reached down and fought for control of the six-gun. He locked his fingers around the grip and struggled desperately with Balestine's hand to pull the pistol from the holster; he was weakening from lack of air. Finally, with a frantic surge of strength, Abe got control, pulled the pistol from its place. Though Balestine tried to stop him, he managed to raised it. He fired at the first target he spotted; Balestine's right foot, protruding out from between his legs— BOOM.

"AWWW." Balestine's howl echoed hollow through the trees and was absorbed into the ugly darkness of the night.

Abe push himself away from Balestine's weakened grip. Drained of strength, Abe struggled to his feet. Balestine, face in agony, was up on one knee, almost standing. Abe pulled back and slammed the Colt into the side of Balestine's head, causing a deep cut on his check and knocking him out cold.

Abe's throat hurt from the struggle, weakened his voice and would remain sore for more than a week. He seriously contemplated putting a bullet in Balestine's head to rid the world of his wretched hide; however, the thought and image of him swinging at the end of a rope, changed his mind and suited his conscience better.

Balestine was still out, when Abe pulled off his left boot. The bullet had past clean through, boot and foot. He shackled Balestine's foot back up, then cleaned and bandaged the wound.

Abe had just finished his work, when Balestine started coming around. "Hmmm…," he moaned weakly, "You decent man, Abie. Had to try, ya know. I'da kilt you, and you still fix me up. Good… thanks."

Abe gave a cockeyed smile, his voice hoarse and shallow, "I want you to be healthy when they hang you."

"Not hanged up yet, Abie. We'll see."

"You'll hang."

At least the snow had stopped when Abe rolled the wagon into Credence, a little before noon. Balestine, shackled and hands tied securely with rope, was in the back. Abe,

132

pushed the break hard with his foot and parked the wagon in front of the Jail. He climbed down, tied off the team and went to the back of the wagon. He removed the tailgate, reached in and literally dragged Balestine out. Once on the ground he shoved him toward the Jail house door, forcing him to limp and wince stiffly through the doorway into the office.

AJ's face was buried in his palms, he looked up with a surprised expression as Balestine stumbled through the door, with Abe close behind.

"What the hell…? Is this the murderin' devil you've been after. He don't look like much."

"He ain't. Lock him up secure, he's a vicious slippery snake."

"Yeah," replied AJ. He snatched the keys out of his desk drawer and shoved Balestine into the first cell, slammed the strap-iron door and locked it. AJ returned to his desk and literally threw the keys back in the drawer and then eased himself slowly back into his chair. The actions and scowl on AJ's face told Abe something was curiously wrong, but Abe figured if AJ wanted share it, he would.

"I'd strongly suggest that, you, me, or

Lanny, be here on guard all the time, until Balestine is convicted and hung."

A distasteful, calloused grin formed on AJ's face. "Lanny? Yeah, right."

"What's up here, AJ?"

"Lanny bit a bullet this mornin'."

"What do you mean, AJ?"

"I mean, Lanny stuck the barrel of his six-gun in his mouth and blew out the top of his head."

"But w...? Tanner's death; he blamed himself?"

"Yeah, that's what he told Connie, this mornin' as he sat on the edge of her bed, before he pulled the trigger. He hadn't done nothin' but get drunk and lay with her, down at the Lucky Loser, since you left for Arland."

AJ gritted his teeth and shook a fisted finger at Balestine. "And, it's all that dirty pukes fault." AJ jerked his .45 Colt out of its holster and fired toward the jail cell. If it hadn't been for the thick iron strapping on the door, Balestine would be dead. However, the bullet glanced off the door and implanted itself deep into the heavy wood overhead beam above the iron cage. This action seemed to quiet AJ's rage, as he holstered his pistol and relaxed back in the chair.

"We-l-l," Abe said coolly, "that almost saved a length of good hemp rope and deprive me of the pleasure of seeing him swing."

AJ's eyes relaxed and he snorted, "That's why I missed.

"I wasn't sure you'd make it back. But, I'm glad you did. It's gonna take a lot to keep that vermin from being lynched, lot of people around here are pretty angry about these murders. I'm not so sure I want to prevent it anyway. If I wasn't wearin' this badge, I'd probably be leadin' the lynch party. Ever' bodies pretty well ticked off about Jenny's murder.

"By the way, there's been some Indian fella, calls himself, Bone, lookin' for you. Came limpin' in here yesterday mornin', says he's your deputy? Said, if you showed up, he'd be down at the Lucky Loser."

"Bone's here? I'll be damned. He'll be a lot of help, if he's up to it.

"Real sorry about Lanny, I should have been more sympathetic and spent some time with him that day I left."

"Wasn't any fault of yers, wouldn't have change anything. He just let it get to him. He was just too young to understand that kind of situation and experience the grief."

"Well, maybe. Just one more death Balestine's responsible for. I'll be glad when he's hanged and done for."

"Yeah. Me too."

"So, Bone made it up here. If you're alright here for now, I think I'll go down and see if I can find him. Besides, I need a drink, or two, maybe more."

"I'm good, go ahead. Hey, don't be too long, I wanna go home and get somethin' to eat."

"Yeah, I can do that." Abe opened the door, looked back AJ, and pointed at Balestine lying on a cot in the cell, "Watch that no-good, don't trust him within arm's length, he's tricky, almost killed me last night."

"If he tries anything, I'd be happy to shoot him and put him out of our misery."

Abe pulled the door shut slow and headed for the Lucky Loser Saloon.

Abe, spotted Bone right off. He was sitting by a window at a table with a bottle of Canadian in front of him, sipping a cup of coffee. He was focused on looking out the window and didn't seem to notice Abe come in and walk to the bar.

At the bar Abe told Milo to give him a cup of coffee.

"Yer the second person to order coffee this time of day. After, I wouldn't serve that Injun over there whisky, he wanted coffee. Didn't see nothin' wrong with that, as long as he didn't stand at the bar."

"Where'd he get the Canadian then?"

"Went out and brought it in himself. He looks too rough for me to tangle with, so I ain't sayin' nothin'. If you want to enforce some law about Injun's drinkin' whisky, go ahead."

"Naw, just give me the coffee and a bottle of Canadian. If you got one open, that would be fine."

"Huh... yeah, shore thing."

Milo brought the coffee and an almost full bottle of Canadian whisky. Abe paid for it and walked over to the table and sat down across from Bone.

"We-l-l, what's so damned interesting out there?"

Without turning his attention from the widow, Bone answered, "You know Abe, you might be surprised what you can notice, if you would observe and not ask so many questions. For instance, I already got us a bottle of Canadian."

"I figgered two was better than one. And, do you suppose Curly Joe Richards and Shorty

Stanton, are here to join the party?"

Bone turned and looked at Abe across the table. "So, you did notice. We-l-l, they got their guns hanging low for some reason. Depends, what party is that?"

"The Stockman's Protection League's party. They don't care much for the smaller rancher's around here. So, they have been gathering a bunch of gunmen and killer's, like Balestine, to eliminate them. I figure there's gonna be a showdown soon between, them and the small ranch hold-outs. Gonna be a lot of blood when it happens."

"You bring Balestine in today?"

"Yeah. Got'm hole up in the Jail till they get a court trial together."

"I thought maybe, you would just kill him when you caught up with him?"

"I seriously thought about it. Law says he should go to trail and hang. So, I thought I should stay within those parameters.

"So, you've met AJ? We need to help him keep Balestine from bein' lynched."

"Why? Waste of good manpower and time."

"Maybe, but were gonna do it anyway."

"Yeah, thought we would."

"What the heck are you doin' up here anyway? I thought I told you to head back to

Arizona?"

"I am a good healer, and, I knew you needed me to cover your back."

"I appreciate it, but I got it done."

"He is not hung yet."

"True."

Abe Wallace: U.S. Federal Marshal

17

Abe and Bone left the saloon and visited with AJ about setting up a watch at the Jail to protect Balestine from any lynch party. Abe and Bone took the first watch of four hours, and sent AJ home to eat and rest.

Abe checked and loaded his slide action, Colt Lightning rifle, and set it across the desk. He then checked the action on his Army .44. After that he propped his feet up on the desk, leaned back in the chair and cat napped. Bone took a .10-gauge coach gun from the wall rack and wiped it down, then loaded it. He also cleaned and readied his old Remington conversion.

AJ, returned a few minutes before six. He brought some beef stew and biscuits his wife had made for everyone to eat. "I hate to give that killer anything good, but, I reckon givin' him food is something I gotta do."

"Yeah," agreed Abe. "'fraid so, AJ. At least he'll be healthy when they hang 'em."

After everyone finished eating, Abe and Bone went to the saloon, leaving AJ alone to sit with the prisoner.

Though a little curious as to why there

wasn't the usual amount of ranch hands at the Lucky Loser, they gave it little mind. The two of them bellied up to the bar and ordered their usual, Canadian and coffee; Abe also asked for a cigar.

The barkeep, brought two cups of coffee, a bottle and the cigar. He handed Abe the cigar, sat the coffee in front of each of them, and the Canadian in front of Abe. "Listen," said the barkeep, "It don't make me no never mind. But, an Injun at the bar will cause trouble around here. It would be appreciated if you two took a table."

"We-ll..," started Abe.

Bone interrupted him. "No... it is alright. I understand. I just as soon sit anyway, my leg is still a little weak."

"If your right with it, then who am I to push the subject." Abe bit the end off of the cigar and spit it to the side, lit it with a match that the barkeeper had laid on the bar. Then, he picked up his coffee and the bottle and went to the table they had sat at before. Bone pulled up a chair and sat down across from Abe.

The two were on their second cup of coffee, half the bottle was gone, when two cowboys that were teasing a saloon girl, happened to notice Bone drinking with Abe. The tall one punched his smaller buddy in the shoulder, pointed and said something to him. The two got up, left the girl, and sauntered over to where Abe and Bone were sitting.

"It ain't right for no Injun to drink in here," said the tall cowboy.

"He only looks like an Indian. Besides, he's with me," replied Abe. Bone sat quiet and looked into Abe's eyes. He knew this was going to end in a fight.

"We don't give a hoot'n hell who ya are. It ain't gonna happen today, or any other day fer that matter." Abe stood up, his eyes narrowed as he locked expressions with the tall cowboy, who stood at least four inches taller.

Bone smiled and lifted his coffee cup to his lips to take a drink. The tall cowboy's eyes flamed, he gritted his teeth, reached around Abe, and slapped the cup out of Bone's hand. Abe reacted by slamming the back of his elbow into the cowboy's face. He fell back and crashed to the floor, out cold. The smaller cowboy went for his six-shooter, but found himself looking down the barrel of Bone's Remington.

"You should get your friend up and find someplace else to drink today," said Bone.

The cowboy nodded, holstered his pistol

and helped his friend to his feet. They both staggered out of the saloon.

Abe looked over at the barkeep who was wiping out glasses, he shrugged and continued his work.

Abe and Bone decided to head back to the Jail a little early. They figured they had enough excitement at the saloon for the evening.

When they entered the Jail, they found AJ knocked out, in a cell and Balestine missing. Abe grabbed a ladle full of drinking water out of a bucket and pour it in AJ's face. He shook and jolted back to life. "What the hell's goin' on...awe...where's Balestine?"

"I'd like to ask you the same questions," said Abe, Bone nodded.

"I don't know. I took the slop jar out and emptied it in the outhouse, and on the way back somebody cold-cocked me on my way back."

"Where is the best place to lynch someone?" asked Bone.

"Hay loft hoist, down at the livery stable," replied AJ. "They hung a fella there a couple years ago." Abe grabbed the Lightning, Bone the .10 gauge and AJ pulled another shotgun from the rack and the three rushed out and headed for the back of Credence Livery.

When they arrived at the rear of the livery barn, sure enough, a crowd of about thirty men, mostly all Stockmen League members, led by Masters McFerrin. They were about to hoist up Balestine, who had his hands tied behind his back and a rope around his neck that was through the hoist pulley. Three men were on the rope, they started pulling it up when they saw the three lawmen. Jax, McFerrin's so called new foreman, was the one in front and two other cowboys were helping.

Abe worked the pump action on the Lightning rifle, aimed at Jax and commanded, "Let loose of that rope or catch a bullet, Jax."

The other two men immediately let the rope go, causing Jax to loose his grip, dropping Balestine to his knees gasping for air. AJ and Bone both had their shot-guns cocked and was covering the crowd.

McFerrin spoke up loud and harshly, "This murderer deserves to be hung."

"Mebee so," said AJ, "But, that's for the Court to decide, not the Stockmen's League. Yer all breakin' the law, trying to lynch this man before a trail."

"Why don't you butt out," called Jax as he pulled and cocked his pistol to fire on AJ.

Abe quickly responded with his rifle and

sent a slug into Jax's torso. Jax's eyes widened in shock as he dropped the six-gun and grabbed his belly. He dropped to his knees and fell face first into the dirt.

All the rest of the crowd had their hands on their six-guns, but didn't want to challenge the two scatter guns covering them. Abe aimed from the hip at Curly Joe and Shorty, since they posed the most dangerous threat now.

"Break this crowd up and leave, or we'll arrest the whole bunch of ya," directed AJ. Nodding at Jax on the ground he said, "And, somebody gather up and get that man to the doctor."

The rest of the men started wandering away slowly, mumbling to one another as they left. Curly Joe and Shorty helped Jax to his feet and dragged him down the street to where the doctor's home was.

McFerrin threatened, "That scum ain't gonna get away with what he's done. We'll make sure he hangs for slaughtering a whole family."

Balestine, breathing hard, on his knees with his hands tied, crisply smiled at McFerrin, "Thanks," he said in a raspy voice.

"You'll pay, you muderin' son-of-a-gun," promised McFerrin.

"You maybe, do paying too," returned Balestine. McFerrin, snorted and started walking away.

Abe went over to Balestine. "Can you stand and walk or do you need a doctor?"

"I am good. Salmon is strong man, my friend."

"Once again, you ain't no damned friend of mine. We only came here to uphold the law. Not to save your mangy ass. Nobodies, gonna lynch my prisoner, not even if it is you."

"All dee same, you save me my life twice, now. I owe you. When they hang me right, it quick? Not choking and gasping at the air."

"All you owe me, is to see your boots swinging in the wind; on the gallows, ordered by the law. Proper like."

"We will see. I just might help out, Abie."

Abe was captivated by what Balestine's said, but not enough to question it.

Abe Wallace: U.S. Federal Marshal

18

After securing Balestine back in his cell, the three lawmen sat down over coffee and some Canadian, to discuss how they were going to handle the situation as it stood now.

AJ reached back to scratch his head, "Ouch. I don't know who it was that cold-cocked me, but if I find out, I'll sure enough oblige a round of fist."

"I'm thinkin'," said Abe, "We should all stay here, at the Jail, until Balestine's trial is over. Only one of us should leave at a time."

"Humph," nodded Bone, agreeing.

"Well, hell yeah. I think that's a darn good idea. If that gang muster's another lynch mob, there will be more blood than that of today, I'm sure," responded AJ. "With all three of us here, they'll be less likely to take us on."

Fortunately, no other trouble came before the trial. Jax died of his wound the next afternoon after the lynching attempt. Fact was, the town was unusually quiet according to AJ's appraisal.

The trial was on a Thursday afternoon, at the newly constructed courthouse. A seasoned, well respected circuit Judge, presided over the proceedings. He did a good job of keeping order. A young local attorney just starting out, was assigned to represent Balestine's interest. Balestine pleaded guilty to all the charges and despite all the trouble they had had up until the trial, it was a quiet, fair trial. The crowd did try to be unruly a few times, but the Judge fined two cowboys and McFerrin, twenty-five dollars for their outburst and that calmed everything back down.

Despite Balestine's guilty plea to the murders, he would not admit to being hired by the Stockmen's Protection League. Abe, began to feel that Balestine had given up and accepted the inevitable.

Somehow, the town came up with a fair and mostly impartial jury. It only took them about forty-five minutes to decide that Balestine should hang for his dastardly deeds. The Judge ordered gallows to be built, and that he should be, 'hanged by the neck, until he was assuredly dead,' on Saturday at one pm. With that pronouncement, he banged his gavel on the bench and closed the proceedings.

Early, Friday afternoon, AJ was home for dinner and Bone was napping in the office chair. Abe was looking through some new

Wanted Posters, when Salmon called to him. "Abie, come here. I got good trade for you," he said in somewhat of a whisper.

Abe approached the cell cautiously.

"Bring chair over, Abie. We have nice talk."

Abe grabbed a chair and slid it across the floor within a couple feet of the cell and sat down. "What is it you want to talk about? What kind of trade could you have?"

"You, good man, Abie. I like you. Sorry, about what I done to you. I am, who I am. If it feels good at the time, I do it. I know you got hard time getting goods on McFerrin. Here is deal....it gonna be good for you. You bring Salmon, half dozen candy sticks and a Canadian bottle and I give what you need to be guilty McFerrin of paying me."

"I ain't no fool. I can't give a prisoner whisky. And, how do I know you ain't spoofin' me?"

"Come on, Abie. I got to die tomorrow, why lie to you. I tell you Abie, I always have contract signed when I work. Got letter, signed by Masters McFerrin. Two-hundred dollars a head for killing settlement people. No, candy sticks and whisky, no letter."

"Why didn't you say something yesterday. Maybe, you'd have gotten a prison sentence instead of a hanging."

"You good man, Abie. I respect. I very bad, I know it. No cage for Salmon. Like animal? No. Hanging, I deserve. I give you Masters McFerrin, no candy sticks and Canadian, no signed letters for you. You give deal now, it a good deal for you, Abie. O-r…I-I take nap and forget."

Abe stroked his unshaven chin with his thumb and forefinger. "We-l-l, interesting proposition. Alright, but, if you're joshin' me, you know what I'll do, Balestine."

"I not given no josh. I tell you about letter; you will find it where I say."

"We-l-l then, let's hear what you got. Where's this letter."

"I got you word on candy sticks and Canadian?"

"Shore thing, you bet'cha."

"We not shake on it; I know you not trust Salmon that far, again. I trust you word Abie. Under wagon seat, there be a small tin box screwed underneath. Letters, I make all clients sign contract, just in case some try something like hanging Balestine. I said, Masters would do some payin' an' he will."

"Yes, you did, yes you did."

Abe stirred Bone and explained the

conversation he just had with Balestine. "Can you handle everything for a while, whilst I take care of this? Or, would you rather we wait on AJ to come back?"

"If you do not mind if I open up with the shotgun on anyone, besides you or AJ, that comes through the door, sure go ahead."

"I'll be back shortly. Just don't open me up with that .10 gauge when I get back."

"If I am not half asleep, I should not."

"We-l-l, you do have a bad habit of getting shot up when I leave you by yourself, you know?"

"No. That will not happen again."

Abe left, crossed the street and walked the boardwalk down to the livery barn. He opened the door quietly and walked cautiously to where Balestine's wagon was parked inside.

Just like Balestine said, when Abe looked under the seat, there it was, a shallow tin box affixed with screws and a leather cover. He untied the leather string latch and pulled out half a dozen envelopes. He opened one with McFerrin's name on it, pulled out and unfolded the letter. There it was, everything he needed to implement Masters McFerrin to Balestine's murders of the small ranches and settlers. The letter did not specify killing men, women or children, just said $200 a head for settlers and small rancher family members.

When Abe got to the Jail, AJ was back sitting at the desk. "We-l-l my friends," announced Abe, "thanks to ol' Balestine there, we got the evidence to charge McFerrin with conspiracy and accessary to murder."

"What the hell are you talkin' about? And, why did you leave Bone here alone with the prisoner?"

Abe put the letter on the desk, in front of AJ. "That," he said.

"What is it?"

"Just read it."

AJ pulled the letter out of the envelope and looked it over. "Well, I'll be damned. Where'd you come across this?"

Abe gave Bone a curious look. "Didn't you tell him."

Bone shrugged, "No."

Abe shook his head and explained about the deal he made with Balestine and then said, "I don't think we should confront McFerrin until after the hanging."

"If you think that's best, then let's do it that way. Looks like from this letter," AJ held up the letter and waved it, "Master's was the only one connected with hiring Balestine. If that's the case then the rest of the Stockmen's League ain't gonna be too happy about this business of murderin' women and children."

"I was thinkin' the same thing, AJ."

19

Salmon devoured the candy sticks immediately, like a little boy that pocketed them from the store. However, he only sipped a little of the Canadian that night.

It was Saturday morning, and though the town was starting to swell in population, things remained surprisingly quiet. Most gathered in the saloons, while some milled around the newly built gallows which had been built, ironically, in the lot behind livery, not twenty-five feet from where they had tried to lynch him just a few days before.

At 10 o'clock, the stage rolled in, Sheriff Linton Haskell stepped down onto the street, the crisp morning air filled his nostrils and cleared his lungs of the musty stench from inside the enclosed coach, as he surveyed the town. AJ had received no word about his coming. AJ, had however, been doing his duty keeping the Sheriff updated on the situation going on between the two factions and the murders. So, at about 10:15, the three lawmen were a bit surprised, when Haskell pushed open the door to the Jail House. And, Sheriff Haskell was even more surprised when he stepped in and found three six-guns, cocked and readied, pointing at him.

"Well men," the Sheriff said, "though I do appreciate your enthusiasm, I don't appreciate your quickness to act hastily, at the drop of the hat. One of you might've shot me."

Abe retorted, "Yeah, might've. However, if any of us had acted hastily, as you put it; you'd be dead in the doorway."

"This is US…"

Sheriff Haskell, held up his hand and stopped AJ in the middle of his sentence. "Yes— US Marshal, Abraham Francis Wallace."

"You can call me, Marshal Wallace. My friends call me, Abe. Not many know my whole name though."

"I know who, and what, is going on in my County."

"Is that a fact?"

"Count on it, Marshal."

Abe and AJ had holstered their pistols, but Bone's was still trained on Sheriff Haskell.

The Sheriff nodded toward Bone and gave him an ill-tempered look, he asked, "And, who might this hard and disrespectful looking individual be? Is he going to shoot me, or what?"

"O-h, him?" smiled Abe, "To the contrary Sheriff, he's got a lot of respect for peace-officers. He's just not as trusting as I am. This is, Blood Bone, my appointed, Special US Deputy Marshal. You can put it away now Bone." Bone nodded and slowly slipped the Remington in place.

AJ asked, "What brings you in, Sheriff Linton?"

"I don't know why you are surprised. Don't you think hanging the worst murderin' son-of-a-bitch in the County's history is the responsibility of the, County Sheriff?

"Besides, I haven't visited with my ol' school chum, Masters in quite a while."

"We-l-l," said AJ, "About your ol' pal McFerrin."

"NO," said Abe, "Don't. Not now, after the hanging."

"AJ, tell me, what about Masters? Tell me, that's an order."

Abe's expression soured, as he pierced AJ with his look.

"We-l-l sir, he…, ah, formed a lynch party and we had to shoot a man. That's taking the law into his own hands. We…we were just wonderin', whether or not to arrest him?"

"Well, I can understand your concern.

And, that's not good. I'll tell you what; don't make it a concern of yours. I will talk to Masters and get it ironed out."

"Okay Sheriff, I'll step back, and let you handle it."

Abe, shot AJ a short smile. Bone, raised an eyebrow and looked off to the side.

"We-l-l fellas, it looks to me like you got everything under control here, so, I'm going down to the Lucky Loser, and visit with some old friends. And, of course, I'll be back in time to escort, that ass over there, to his doom."

Balestine, had been watching and listening to the whole conversation since the Sheriff had come in. It was pretty obvious he had formed a negative opinion of the Sheriff. "You not nut'ting, lawmans," he said. "You would no make patch on dee ass of Abie's britches."

"Well, we'll see just how cocky you are when you start up those steps to the gallows." With that, the Sheriff turned and left.

The Sheriff hadn't notice, because he knew nothing of Balestine, but he was feeling the Canadian, for he had polished off the rest of the bottle in just the last hour.

At 12 o'clock, the local Preacher came and offered to pray with Balestine.

"You go an' pray for youself," said Balestine, "Salmon, know where he goin'. Mebee, I meet you there, preacher man," he smirked.

"May God condemn your everlasting soul to the fiery pit forever," replied the Preacher.

"Yeah, you also Preacher mans."

The Preacher slammed his Bible shut and left in a huff. As soon as he left, slamming the door behind him, the three men glanced at each other and slowly chuckled and soon were almost uncontrollably laughing.

At 12:30 AJ, took a set of shackles and locked them to Balestine's hands and ankles. No sooner had he got done with that, the Sheriff returned.

"Alright fellas," he started off, "here is how were going to do this. Everyone grab a rifle out of the rack and check the load. Make sure your six-shooters are ready too. Then at 10 minutes of, me and Marshal Wallace will take the lead, me on the left and you on the right, Marshal."

"No," said Abe firmly, "Hell no."

"No, what do you mean, no?"

"I mean no," Abe stepped forward, within two feet of Haskell's face, "no, that's not the way we're gonna do things. You've talked enough, now it's my turn. First, Balestine's not your prisoner, he's mine. Bone and me have followed him all the way up from Arizona. I went after him, and caught him, out of your jurisdiction. And no, I ain't grabbing a rifle out of the rack." Abe reach over and slid the Lightning from the desk and jerked the action sending a shell into the chamber. "I have my own. You carry what you want Sheriff, but Bone and AJ are gonna carry the coach guns. Bone, you'll be front left and I'll be back left."

"Abe," Bone nodded

"AJ, you front right. And Sheriff, if you want to join us, then you'll be back right. Now, let's see to it this gets carried out smooth and proper. If you want Sheriff, you can slip the rope over him. That will give you something to brag about, next election."

"Alright," agreed Sheriff Haskell. "I think, that just might be better, we'll do it your way. And, I was appointed, not elected."

"Figgers, and damned you will. Now, let's go. Sheriff, you'll do the actual hanging, that is if you got the stomach for it."

"Yeah, yeah, I got that covered."

So, at 10 minutes to the hour Abe opened the door to the cell. "Well Balestine, it's time to go."

"Sure Abie, I ready. How 'bout you Mr. Sheriffs? Hee-hee."

"Damned right, you scum. On your way."

The five filed out, just like Abe had ordered, and started the same walk they had made to stop the lynching.

"Abie, thank you. Think we made a good trade?"

"Well yeah, I think so. I'm gonna take care of it, soon after we get this done."

"You do good, Abie."

Haskell cocked his head with a mean curious look. "What the hell is he goin' on about?"

"Not something you wanna know about right now, Sheriff. You'll know soon enough, and I hope you're dedicated to your job."

"What, of course I am."

The group turn the corner at the livery to face a large crowd of, maybe, two-hundred people. They started parting to let the group through, and as they headed toward the gallows, many spit and struck Balestine with their fist. When they were within a few feet of the stairs to the gallows, some did not want to step aside. Abe made a powerful shove with the Lightning, pushing a couple of cowboys to the ground. Abe started up the steps first AJ behind him. Balestine was next and Sheriff Haskell behind him; Bone was last.

Abe was ready to step on the platform when Balestine stopped about halfway up, turned and swung his wrist shackles around Sheriff Haskell's neck. Then, being two steps up from the Sheriff, he pushed his foot on his shoulder, turning him much like he had Abe a few days earlier. Balestine pulled the chain powerfully tight around Haskell's neck. Haskell, who was seconds away from death dropped his rifle and collapsed on the steps.

Abe, shoved past AJ on his way down; when he got to the two men, he started smashing Balestine on the side and top of his head with all he had with the Lightning. Balestine was a strong man with unbelievable endurance, but he finally collapsed. Him and Sheriff Haskell, both slid down the stairs to the bottom of the steps, limp and unconscious, there at Bone's feet.

Suddenly, Balestine's eyes popped open and he came back to life and started to stand up. Bone, drew back and smacked him in the face with the butt of the coach gun. Balestine, fell back landing on top of the Sheriff. Abe, had worked his way down to the bottom where Bone was. He untangled the chain from around

Haskell's neck and grabbed Balestine by his shirt and pulled him up and tossed him aside.

"Dammit, somebody get the Sheriff a doctor," Abe yelled at the crowd.

Men in the front of the crowd pulled a man forward and shoved him toward Abe. "Here's the doctor," they said.

The man had a small black bag and he rushed to Sheriff Haskell and examined his neck closely. "I am sorry," he said. "Nothing, I can do for the Sheriff, his wind pipe is crushed. He's gone."

The doctor, started to examine Balestine wounds, Abe grabbed the shoulder of his coat, pulling him away. "He don't need no fixin'.

"Someone, get me a bucket of water."

Two or three men went to a water trough behind the livery barn, one found a bucket. Another man snatched it out of his hand and scooped it full in the trough. Then he ran it over and handed it to Abe.

Abe took the bucket full on water and threw it in Balestine's face. Balestine, shook violently and came to. Abe put his rifle in his left hand and grabbed the wrist shackles in the middle of the chain with his right, and literally dragged Balestine up the stairway to the platform.

"That's the last damned murder you'll commit on this earth," Abe breathlessly said.

Abe tightened the slack out of chain and put his foot in Balestine's torso and held him there until he caught his breath. After a bit, Abe removed his foot, leaned the Lightning against a corner of the rail around the platform and pulled Balestine to his feet. He stood him under the hangman's noose, pulled it tight around his neck.

Abe stepped back a couple steps and said, "Salmon Balestine, you've been convicted of numerous murders by a jury of your peers and sentenced to hang by the neck until dead. Do you have any last words?"

Balestine's face was a bloody mess, his nose was broken and his lips were swelled and bleeding, he also had a gash on one side of his head and his ear was torn. He spits blood at the crowd and said, "I meet you all, at dee gates a hell."

"Is that it?" asked Abe.

"Thanks Abie, you good man. I showed that Sheriff's cocky, didn't..." Balestine never finished what he was saying, because Abe, pulled back the lever on the drop gate of the gallows. When Balestine hit the bottom of the slack in the rope with a pop, the crowd cheered and shouted as they shook their fist at the dead man at the end of the rope.

Abe ordered a few men to take the Sheriff to the undertakers. Masters McFerrin took charge of that saying, "I'll make funeral arrangement for him."

"That might be one funeral you don't attend," said Abe.

"What are you talkin' about, Wallace?"

"O-h, you'll know soon." Abe and the rest walked away without any further talk.

20

Back at the Jail the stove still had some warmth to it, so they all poured a cup of coffee.

Abe took a sip of his coffee as he stood by the stove and said, "That was a god-damned circus. Just ain't right the Sheriff died like that."

"Didn't think you cared much for the Sheriff, Abe?" questioned AJ.

"He was an officer of the law and a man doing what he thought was right. Dying in the hands of a man like Balestine is a dog-gone travesty."

"Well," said AJ, "He wasn't one of my favorite men. But, when you put it like that, I have to agree."

Bone shook his head, "Humph."

"What do you think we otta do about the letter, Abe?" asked AJ.

"We-l-l, I believe the Judge is still in town, I hope. He's staying at the Lucky Loser ain't he?"

"I think so, yeah," replied AJ.

"Take the letter down and find the Judge, and see if he won't swear a warrant for, Masters McFerrin."

"You shore we should do that now?"

"No time like the present. Let's get this done and over with. Keep it discreet, we don't want the whole darn town up in arms."

AJ, left the office to get the warrant. Abe fell into the desk chair and pick up the Lightning. He examined the desk drawer until he found the one with a rag and some oil. He put a bit of oil on the rag and started cleaning Balestine's blood off of it. Bone went to a jail cell and laid on a cot, pulled his hat down over his eyes and was asleep in less than a minute.

AJ, had been gone about a half-hour when he threw open the door. Smiling large, waving a paper in his hand, he said, "Got it. And, the Judge said if we prove the signatures match, he would stay in town and conduct a trial of conspiracy and murder against McFerrin."

"Alright then," said Abe, "let's take a walk down to Stockmen's Hall and kick in the door and drag his sorry ass down here."

"Wait," said AJ. "We don't have any comparison to the signature on Balestine's letter."

Bone, was standing in the doorway of the Jail cell unnoticed. As he pushed his hair back with one hand, and sit his hat on his head with the other, sleepy-eyed he said, "Bet he has got some kind of signature on a document over at the bank."

"We-l-l, heck yes," said AJ.

"Good thinking, Bone," Abe said. "You're the chief peace-officer around here now, AJ. Why don't you see if you can catch somebody at the bank before it closes and get something we can look at."

AJ, looked at the clock on the wall, "The bank closes in ten minutes. I gotta go." He turned and dashed out the door, slamming it on his way.

Sloan Hope, the president of the bank was pulling the double doors shut as AJ jumped up on the boardwalk. "Wait Sloan," AJ called out.

"Bank's closed for business for today, Deputy. It will have to wait till Monday morning at eight-o'clock. I got a Stockmen's meeting to get to."

"This is one Stockmen's meeting you just might want to miss, Sloan."

"What makes you say that?"

"I got a warrant inside my coat pocket for Masters McFerrin's arrest, that's why. I need you to open the bank, so I can get some evidence."

"Masters McFerrin? Why on earth would

you have a warrant for Masters? And, what does the bank got to do with anything?"

"Right now, that's the laws business. I'm sure you'll find out soon enough. Now, open up the bank; I need a document with Masters McFerrin's signature on it."

"I don't know about this. Bank documents are private and…"

"Either open this door," AJ interrupted, "or, you and me are goin' down to the Lucky Loser and visit the Circuit Judge. I'm sure you don't want to be charged with accessory to murder. But hell, if that's what you want, let's head down the street."

"Murder? No. No… I will open it." Sloan fumbled around with the keys and pushed the door open. "Over here," he said.

Sloan went to an office cabinet, opened the second drawer from the top and thumbed through a couple folders. "Here's something. I think this might work. It's a quick claim deed for a ranch Masters bought a month ago after the folks that owned it left hastily."

"Yeah, that will do," said AJ. "Let me see it."

"You sure this is legal?"

"Shore. Besides, if it ain't, it's my responsibility, not yours."

"Alright, I got to get the bank closed now."

"Don't go to that meeting, I'm warning you."

"Well, why?"

"Cause, we're goin' down to the Stockmen's Hall presently and arrest Masters McFerrin, for murder."

"Got it," AJ said as he entered through the door.

"Good," replied Abe. "We-l-l. fellas, let's go serve this warrant."

AJ, pulled a Winchester rifle from the wall rack. As he checked the load, he said, "I'm thinkin', we had better go down there expecting a fight."

"Yeah, I'm thinking you're right," replied Abe.

As usual Bone nodded.

Everyone checked their guns; Bone, also took a rifle from the wall rack. Abe checked the action and load of his Colt Army and picked up the Lightning.

"Better take a set of wrist shackles with us AJ."

"Yep," replied AJ, so he pulled a pair out of the bottom desk drawer of the desk.

21

The Stockmen's Protection League Hall, was a large, well-built, log cabin with fine fitted corners, and a shake roof. Probably the most stable and secure building around town. If Masters chose to make a stand, it would not be easy to get him or anyone making a stand with him, out. There was only one door, a wide, thick heavy sawn wood door. Only two windows, both in front, with thick shutters that could be pulled shut from the inside over the glass windowpanes. The door had a six inch square, slide opening, so as to see who was at the door from the inside.

The hall was a little outside of town, west, next to the main road. Six horses stood tied to the hitching rail and two buckboard wagons were setting in front of the hall. It was spitting snow now, and the temperature had dropped well below freezing, so there was a stream of smoke pouring out of the stone chimney at one end of the building.

Though, it was some quarter of a mile away from the Jail, the three well-armed men, chose to walk the distance. As they walked, leaning into the cruel winter wind, similar thoughts of the past events that lead to this, pictured vividly in each of their minds. The showdown that they all had been anticipating was here and they were ready. This would be the final accounting for all the blood that had been spilled.

When they stood in front of the Stockmen's Protection League Hall, AJ suggested, "You fellas stay here and back me up. I'll go up and serve this warrant. No one can shoot me standing at the door." Both, Abe and Bone nodded.

There was a light layer of snow on the ground, now it was starting to accumulate fast. AJ started walking the twenty feet to the door. He had the shackles in his left hand and his rifle in the other. A board porch with no top was in front of the door. Hitching rails were at each end of the porch, with a watering trough and pump behind the one on the right. The pump had a frozen stream of ice running from the spout to the two inch thick layer of ice in the trough, a wooden water bucket sat upside down next to the pump.

AJ stepped up onto the porch and banged on the door with the shackles, then he laid the rifle across the crook in his left arm. The little slide popped open, a nose and mouth appeared in it. "AJ, what do you want? This is a closed meeting."

AJ recognized the voice, but couldn't identify who it was. "This is official business. I am afraid, I'm gonna break yer meeting up today. I have a warrant for Masters McFerrin's arrest. Either send him out or let me in," he ordered.

"For what?" said the surprised voice.

"For murder and conspiracy to commit murder."

"I...I will tell him."

"Tell him, I got proof. I got a letter signed by him to Balestine. He hired him to kill farmers and small ranchers for two-hundred dollars a head."

The voice replied, "That's hard to believe. I want no part of this, if that's true."

"It's true, shore enough. Tell him to come out. The rest of you come out also."

The little door slide closed. A few minutes past, and Jim Walker, a cattle rancher and the voice at the door, stepped out. "Masters says he ain't comin' out. If you want him, you'll have to come in and get him, he ain't givin' up without a fight. That's what he said; I want out of this. I had no idea, and I don't want anything to do with this. There's other good men in there that want to come out too."

"Tell them they got ten minutes to make up their minds. After that, we're comin' in shootin'."

Walker, stepped back inside, leaving the door open and repeated what AJ had just said. Walker stepped back out and started to close the door. A shot from inside splintered the door frame, just missing Walker.

AJ and Walker bent down and headed for cover behind one of the wagons parked out front. Before, Jim Walker could fully hide himself behind the wagon, a shot fired from one of the open, shuttered windows of the hall, hit him full in the back. Walker dropped to his knees and fell face first into the fresh snow, he was dead. Another shot, fired from the same window, went through the wooden sideboard of the wagon and hit AJ in the right shoulder, causing him to drop his rifle in the snow. He crawled behind the back wheel of the wagon and drew his pistol. He aimed carefully and fired three shots at the open widow. The last two hit there mark, a man's voice bawled out after the second shot, "I'm hit," said someone inside. The third shot apparently took out whoever it was shooting from the window. All was quiet now.

Abe and Bone, had taken cover behind a

stand of dead lilac bushes, next to a large cottonwood tree. They both started firing at the windows and the door. AJ, reached out and pulled his rifle over. He chambered a shell, and started firing at the window where Walker had be shot from. Shots were coming back at them from both windows.

"Save your ammunition," Abe shouted. "Hold up AJ. How bad you hurt?"

"Not too bad. The sideboard slowed the bullet down. It's still in my shoulder though, not deep. Hurts like hell, I'm okay for now."

"If we cover you, can you make over here?"

"I think so."

"Then come ahead.

"Bone, let's not let AJ get shot." Bone gave his usual nod.

AJ raised up a bit, keeping ducked down, he started running zig-zag toward the cottonwood. Abe and Bone, blazed their rifles at both the widows. There was no way anyone from inside could get off a shot until AJ reached the cottonwood.

"Let me look at that shoulder," said Bone.

AJ, painfully pulled off the right side of his coat. Bone pulled out a folding knife from his pocket, opened it and cut away AJ's shirt from around the wound and look at it closely. Then he reached down and grabbed a handful of snow and slapped it on the bullet wound. Before, AJ had a chance to react, Bone popped the bullet out of his shoulder with the thin blade of the pocket knife.

"Dam Bone!" AJ yipped.

"Put more snow on it and your coat back on. That will suffice until you get a doctor to look at it."

"Well, I guess I ought to say thanks," said AJ.

"Yes, go ahead."

"Okay then," growled AJ, "Thanks."

"Short of burnin' the place down," said Abe, "I don't see how we can get them out of there. Bone nodded.

AJ said, "It's too darn cold out here to wait until they run out of ammunition."

"Look," said Bone, pointing at the cabin door.

Someone was waving a white cloth on the tip of a rifle barrel. "What do you want," called Abe.

Curly Joe was the one waving the flag and he stepped out on the porch. "Hey Wallace, some of us ain't in on this deal. We want to come out, we ain't done nothin'."

"Alright," called Abe. "Those of you who

want to come out, do so with your weapons held over your heads. Don't make no sudden moves or it'll be your last."

Eight men exited in a hurry, the last one out the door was Curly Joe. "Curly, holster your pistol and come on over here. The rest of you, get on your wagon or your horse and go home."

The seven men wasted little time complying with Abe's instructions, they all put leather to their animals and left like their tail ends were on fire. Three horses remained tied to the rail. Curly holstered his six-gun and walked over to where Abe and the others were. The snow had stopped, but the temperature had drop considerably. When the men talked, their breaths was so thick they could hardly see each other's faces.

"We-l-l Wallace, you certainly wrapped this one up nice and tidy, didn't ya?"

"Not quite yet. Who's left in there?"

"Masters and his new foreman, Max somethin' or another."

"What about Shorty?"

"Someone out here, picked him off at the window. After, he shot that fellow in the back."

"You're usually loyal to your employer to a

fault, Curly. How come you didn't stick it out?"

"We-l-l, yer right about that. But, I know a lost cause when I see one. Besides, wasn't a 'nough money in it for a unwinnable standoff."

"Well AJ," said Abe, "there any reason to detain Curly here?"

"None, I can think of."

"Curly," asked Abe, "you know anything about Masters deal with Balestine?"

"Hell no. I wouldn't have anything to do with that murderin' mad man."

"One of those horses up there, yours?"

"Yeah, the big bay."

"If you want, go get him. But Curly, don't leave town until this is over, understand?"

"I tell you what, I'll leave him for now. I'll just walk down to the saloon and come back after you get this done. Just to let you know, Master's has no intention of given up. He's punishing himself for that family Balestine slaughtered. I ain't up to bein' no martyr. That Max fella, loyal, like an old dog sittin' at his feet. So, al'm figgerin' yer gonna have to kill'm both."

"Alright Curly, thanks. Oh, one more thing, Curly. What about this foreman, Max. Is he involved in any murders?"

"Hell Abe, how would I know?"

"Yeah, you wouldn't tell me if you did."

Curly started out toward the saloon.

"Well," said AJ, "I don't know how we're gonna get those two outa there, short of torchin' the place. Any ideas Abe?"

Abe, looked around to see if Bone, had any suggestions. But he was gone. "Where's Bone?"

AJ twisted his head back and forth. "I don't know. He was here a minute ago."

Abe looked up toward the hall and said, "Look AJ. On the roof."

Bone was on the roof of the hall, he had the wooden bucket in his right hand. He stepped carefully across the roof toward the chimney at the end of the building. The shakes were slippery because of the ice that had formed on the roof. When he reached the chimney, Bone turned the bucket upside down and fitted it tightly over the clay insert pipe. Then he disappeared back over the other side. A minute or so later he reappeared from around the end of the building to run sig-zag back to where AJ and Abe were.

Watching Bone on the roof, AJ had got careless about his cover. A rifle shot from the window on the right, sent a second bullet through AJ's right shoulder, close to the first wound. He buckled at the knees, Abe and Bone caught him before he hit the ground. They lowered him down easy into a layer of fresh snow on the ground.

"Hold on there, AJ," Abe said.

"Yeah. I didn't expect that. Hell, not my day."

"The bullet went right through," said Bone. "Painful, but it is not serious if we stop the bleeding and keep the wound clean."

"Think you can walk, AJ?"

"Shore, but I ain't goin' no-wheres, Abe. Help me up. I'm gonna see this through."

22

Abe and Bone helped AJ to his feet. They leaned him against the cottonwood and pulled his pistol out and handed it to him.

The tree was huge with two large main branches growing out of one trunk from the ground. It provided excellent cover for the three of them. Now, they turned their attention back toward the hall. Smoke was flowing in a circular motion from the window and back into the cabin. The shutters were open more than half-way now. This was the same window that all the shooting had been coming from. Abe chambered a shell into the Lightning and rested his left elbow against the trunk of the tree.

"Bone," said Abe, "Aim your rifle at the center of the opening between that set of shutters. AJ, you do the same with your pistol. I'll count three; when I do, start firing until your guns are empty."

Bone gave his usual nod and AJ said, "Okay?" curiously.

"One- Two- THREE." BOOM- BANG- BOOM- BOOM. Somewhere in the middle of about thirty to thirty-five rounds being fired, someone yelled, "OH-H, I've been…AWWWW." The firing stopped and everything was silent. The shutters and the window glass were splintered and shattered to pieces. They all started reloading their weapons.

AJ who was having a tough time reloading said, "That wasn't Masters voice. Whoever it was, is prob'ly done."

"That was the plan," said Abe.

Masters voice called from the window. "Listen, Max is hurt bad. Get the doctor down here for him."

"Sure, as soon as you come out, with your hands empty and high in the air," Abe returned.

"No, I ain't givin' up."

"Then, no deal," returned Abe. "Be your fault if he dies. Give it up, you don't have a chance,"

There was no answer for a long moment, then, "Alright, I don't want Max to die. I'm comin' out."

"Unarmed Masters. I mean what I am sayin' now," called Abe.

The door swung open and smoke swirled around the form of Masters. His hands were above his head, but as he stepped out he had a pistol in each hand.

"Drop those damned pistols. NOW, Masters," Abe shouted.

"GO to HELL." The pistol blazed toward the three, and all three returned fire. Masters ran toward them firing and kept pulling the triggers, even after he hit the ground.

As Abe and Bone approached him on the ground the snow was flying again. Masters continued to click the hammers until his arms just dropped.

Abe and Bone were standing over him, his eyes were closed; then they popped open, glowing red and pink, bloodshot around crystal blue. He clicked both the empty pistols one more time. He moaned shallow in a whisper, "I didn't mean for that whole family to die." Masters expired, his eyes wide open.

Abe said, "Wait here Bone. I'm gonna see what's going on inside." Bone nodded.

Abe stepped through the door cautiously. The room had layers of thin blue smoke drifting all through the cabin. A man was lying motionless on the floor below the window. Abe went over and checked, he was dead; two bullet holes in his face and one through the neck and one in his chest.

The fire in the fireplace was smoldering. It was obvious that someone had thrown a big bucket of water on the fire, the bucket laid on the floor nearby.

Abe, Bone and AJ with his shoulder in a sling, came in through the door of the Lucky Loser Saloon. A blowing blizzard of huge, freezing, white flakes came in with them swirling all around. Abe and Bone struggled to shut the door. They went straight to the bar where a dozen people gathered round and congratulated them on solving the murders and taking care of those who were responsible. Everyone, made over AJ, wanting to know if he was going to be alright. A few even ask if he was going to get the County Sheriff's job. A local politician wanted to make sure he knew he was now acting Sheriff and that he needed to be sworn in.

The crowd wouldn't let any of them, including Bone, buy a drink for themselves. After a few drinks downed, the voice of Curly Joe, sounded behind those at the bar. "Abe Wallace."

All at the bar turned around to see what was up with Curly Joe. He stood holding his coat tail behind his back with his left hand, his right hand was raised loose over his .44 six-shooter.

"What's the deal Curly. This thing is over,

remember?"

"Like you said, I am loyal to my employer. I still got work to do."

"You wanna explain that. Your last employer is dead. He can't pay you if he's dead."

"Already been paid, in advance. So, my work ain't done yet. Before, I left Stockmen Hall, Masters paid me a thousand dollars, cash, to kill you in event he was dead. He's dead, and you will be shortly. Then, my job will be done, and, I can move on."

"Him being dead, and you already got your money, why take the risk? Just move on; let's have a drink and leave this behind. I put your bay up at the livery by the way."

"Thanks for that. You know, I don't work like that. Been paid, so now I'll complete the work."

"We-l-l, if that's the inevitable. Let's get on with it. Why should this be an uncomfortable affair? Let me take my coat off, and you remove yours. I promise, no tricks." Abe's coat was bulky and he knew it would hinder and slow down his action; not a good thing facing a gun-hand like Curly.

"Yeah, we can do that Wallace. Either way, yer a dead man."

Both men removed their coats. Curly tossed his over the back of a nearby chair. Abe handed his to Bone. Bone took the coat and said in low voice, "I heard Curly was fast."

"I know."

"You ready to die, Abe?"

The two side stepped around in a half circle in the middle of the room about six feet from each other, their eyes locked in a penetrating deadly gaze.

As they slowly circled each other, now, less than five feet apart, Abe said, "Gonna be one hell of a funeral for a thousand dollars, Curly. Sure, you don't want to just leave this behind?"

"Can't Abe."

"Yeah, I know."

No one could tell if one or the other man drew first. For a certainty, Abe's Army spoke first, loud and sure. The shot hit Curly full in the chest, a bit left of center. Curly's six-shooter didn't even fire. He was dead before his head pounded back into the floor.

The snow stopped that morning, but it left behind about two foot. Some walkways were shoveled and some were not. Since AJ couldn't shovel around the Jail, Abe and Bone saw to it.

Abe had sent a telegraph message down to

his Captain in Arizona Territory, informing him that the job was done and that he would be heading back as soon as the weather cleared. He also, told him that he had just mailed a full report about the whole thing.

Abe, Bone and AJ were sitting around the fire in the County Jail Office, talking about the past fracas and drinking coffee with a shot of Canadian, of course. Abe mentioned how he couldn't wait to get back to Arizona and the desert. Then the junior telegraph operator pecked at the door. He came in with a message from the Captain. Abe quickly looked it over and cursed under his breath, "Dammit."

"What's up, Abe," inquired AJ.

"Awe hell," snarled Abe, "I got another assignment up here. I am supposed to go see some big cattle rancher up in Billings, Montana about his missing wife as soon as the weather allows.

"I'm tired of this cold, I wanna go back to the desert."

AJ spit a mouth full of coffee on the side of the stove and started choking and laughing uncontrollably. Bone joined in, even though he hardly ever laughed out loud.

"What," said Abe, "You two sound like a bunch of barnyard hens cackling."

Orin Vaughn

Abe Wallace: U.S. Federal Marshal

Other Titles by Orin Vaughn

COLD CREEK JUSTICE

GUNS GRIT N WOMEN I

GUNS GRIT N WOMEN II

CASH & CARREY

89845423R00127

Made in the USA
San Bernardino, CA
09 October 2018